I read the information through twice and try to make the words correspond with my image of Lucas. On the outside he seems so cool and cavalier, and yet on the inside he's all churned up. I now feel very guilty about calling him Luc-Arse and I suddenly want to be his very best friend in the entire world. I'm sure I could fix him with great big Band-Aids of compassion and cheery encouragement. What I lack in information I'll make up for with enthusiasm! I'm so wrapped up in my conviction that for a millisecond I even forget about Toby. That hasn't happened for a while.

Ella Mental

Life, Love, and More Good Sense

Meet Ella Mental in

Ella Mental
And the Good Sense Guide

Ella Mental

Life, Love, and More Good Sense

Amber Deckers

Simon Pulse
New York London Toronto Sydney

SIMON PULSE
An imprint of Simon & Schuster Children's Publishing Division
1230 Avenue of the Americas, New York, NY 10020

Originally published in Great Britain in 2006 by Hachette Children's Books
Published by arrangement with Hachette Children's Books

The text of this book was set in Goudy.
Manufactured in the United States of America
First Simon Pulse edition December 2006
10 9 8 7 6 5 4 3 2 1
Library of Congress Control Number 2006928444
ISBN-13: 978-1-4169-1323-8
ISBN-10: 1-4169-1323-8

For Craig—my love and my light

Chapter 1
Hi ho, Hi ho

My love is as bright and bold and heavenly as the luminous paper stars glued to the ceiling above my bed. I can't contain it. My romance-riddled heart keeps pumping large lumps of delirious devotion from my head to my feet and around and around my body until I'm left feeling wonderfully dizzy and just a tad woozy. And there's not a thing I can do to stop it. Even if I wanted to. Which I definitely do not. It's only been a few weeks and I'm still trying to digest the glorious fact that my best friend Toby—the very same guy I've known and adored since like forever, is now *my boyfriend*!

Lying tucked up in bed with nowhere particular to be, I decide to practice different ways of saying it out loud. I drop the words from my lips quickly and casually, like it's something I was expecting to happen all along. I speak the words slowly and deliberately, like our relationship is monumental and could just change my life forever. I then try emphasizing the *my* (as in "*my* boyfriend"), just to prove that I won't take any flirty floozies messing about and pointing passionate eyeballs at my honey bunch. I even shorten it to "my boyf"—like it's a neat accessory I can carry around with me everywhere. I am a lady in love and I don't mind hollering about it one bit.

Who would have guessed that little Toby and Ella—the same mischievous toddlers whose favorite trick was to rip off their poo-nappies and hide them in dark places (like behind wall units and underneath sofas)—would remain best friends and eventually become an item. I remember the days when I used to make flower stews for Toby like it was just yesterday. It's going to be a beautiful wedding one day.

Today is Saturday, which means that there are sixteen days until Valentine's Day and as it's our first together—AS A COUPLE—I'm planning on doing something very special to show Toby just how much he means to me. And reminiscing about our childhood starts me thinking: I wonder if Mum has any baby photos of the two of us together? What about making Toby a collage of these photos (nothing too cheesy, mind you—just something small in a frame).

There are moments when I tip the genius scales.

The joy of having a laze-about sister is that I'm usually the first one in the bathroom, and by the time I'm finally dressed, shiny, and downstairs, my dear twin Anna is still in her pajamas and just barely managing to remain upright in front of the telly. She's blearily sipping on a hot cup of tea and thinking about waking up, while I'm eagle-eyed and ready to flick through the family photos. Suddenly our dad appears from out of nowhere. The collage will have to wait—I'm much better off at Toby's, where no one gives me chores to do.

"Not so fast, Ella!" Dad says and traffic-cop signals me to do an about-turn.

"Whaaaat?" I groan.

"We're due for a family meeting," he barks, like it's an order, which it is. I know when I'm beaten and so I wordlessly humph my way to the sofa and sit beside Anna, who either hasn't heard Dad or isn't bothered enough to spend the energy on a reaction. She continues testing her tea with her lips and peering at the telly through the crack in her eyelids. Her only flicker of a reaction is when Dad jabs the telly off.

"Norm's son Roger has just been accepted as an

apprentice mechanic," he announces, like Roger just commandeered the first manned spaceflight to Saturn or something. Dad pauses and waits for us to respond with the obvious "So what?" but I won't do him the favor and I think Anna is still trying to work out what happened to the telly. Norm is Dad's best mate, Norm-from-the-pub, and whatever Norm does Dad must go one better. And that goes vice versa for Norm, which means that this situation is suddenly looking very bleak for Anna and me.

"So I've decided," he continues authoritatively, "that it's about time you two started earning your own pocket money. You're almost sixteen and I'm fed up with funding your fun. You need to learn the value of a pound, and the best way to do that is to earn the pound yourself. What you decide to do is up to you, but I'll expect a progress report on your part-time job search one week from today. Are we clear?"

The curtain has gone down on my sister's dumb act and she's suddenly very much awake. We pause, sigh, and nod in dismal unison. Dad appears rather pleased with himself and quickly disappears from the lounge to update Mum, no doubt.

"Well that's just nonsense!" I groan miserably. A job will mean less time with Toby. Typical, just as I get a boyfriend. "Now what?" I turn to Anna.

"Now we get jobs," she sniffs haughtily. "I was thinking about taking up modeling anyway."

"You were what?" I scoff.

"You heard me."

"What sort of modeling?" I ask. "Clay modeling, maybe. Ha ha ha." Except Anna doesn't think I'm very funny at all.

"You're a riot, Ella. Not! I'm talking about photographic modeling and I'm being completely serious. I believe I have what it takes to make it." Anna gives me a snooty stare like I'm a hideous insect she's contemplating swatting. I'm tempted to remind her that we are twins, but then she has got the whole English rose thing going on. And she did get the cheekbones.

"Well good luck, then," I mutter halfheartedly. I know I'm not being very sisterly, but it's just like Anna to be so optimistic about a ruling that could seriously cut into my romance time.

"I'd have thought that you of all people would be supportive," Anna fumes irritably. "If I remember rightly, wasn't it you with your Ella

Mental Nonsense Guide that said that people without dreams don't have anything!"

She has remembered rightly and although I should be feeling rather guilty, as Anna charges off in the direction of the stairs and her bedroom, I can't help noticing that she has a severe case of bed head. It's not easy to take this model talk seriously when she looks like she's been doing headstands on Velcro. And how was I to know that she actually listens when I take the time to share my Good Sense Guide wisdoms with her? Usually she just stares at me with eyes like two glazed doughnuts, so it's difficult to tell. But Anna does have a point. Never laugh at anyone's dreams—that's Good Sense Guide number thirty-something-or-other.

My diary is chock-a-block with Good Sense Guide logic and one of these days I'm definitely going to send it off to someone who'll print it and circulate it for teens everywhere to take a look at. Some people are trainspotters, others are planespotters; I'm a good-sense spotter! I observe the world around me and document my insights in a list called the Good Sense Guide. There's a lot we can learn from life and people around us, except we're all usually too busy bouncing about in our little bubbles to take much notice. But that's what I do. I take notice and turn what I see into very useful and essential bits of clear-cut advice, which is why it's called the *Elemental* Good Sense Guide. My friends say I'm batty and also happen to call me Ella Mental, but this has nothing whatsoever to do with the Good Sense Guide. There is a distinct difference.

My eardrums wobble with the sound of Anna's bedroom door slamming upstairs, which takes me back to Dad's part-time job ultimatum, which gets me thinking once again about how I'd rather be spending all my time with Toby instead of earning my own pocket money, which reminds me that I was on my way to Toby's before Dad called the dreary family meeting. That's called a train of thought, and sometimes mine are so long I completely forget where they're heading.

Chapter 2
A Dog's Life

It takes me exactly thirteen and a half minutes to walk to Toby's and as I approach the familiar, pebble-dashed Sinclair home I notice the empty parking space next to Mrs. T's old burgundy Rover. I know Toby's mum said I should start calling her Pam, but I can't help it—I still call her Mrs. T, which is short for Mrs. Toby. Silly old childhood habits die the slowest deaths. So do childhood memories, it seems—because I still can't get used to the fact that Toby's dad has actually moved in with the blonde non-Mrs. T woman I caught him canoodling with in the Jewel Garden not so long ago. And if I still expect to find his sleek silver MG bullet parked in the drive, I can't even begin to imagine how it must grind Toby up inside.

Imagining Toby moving about somewhere inside the house before me turns my muscles as limp as liquorice laces. We really haven't had very much time together since that unforgettable day we declared our mutual fancy-feelings (and cleared up the whole Beastly Becky/Glen botch-up, where for one brief moment we let meddling strangers get in the way of our true love for one another). Toby, his mum, and his older sister Melanie left shortly thereafter to spend their Christmas holidays with Mrs. T's family in the Algarve. I suppose she felt they needed to get away from it all for a bit, but on a personal level I found it very inconvenient and stressful. My love boat docked but I wasn't permitted to board. How cruel. So it's still very early days for Toby and me and we're still finding our way around this lovey-dovey thing we now have going on. Of course I'm feverishly excited by it all but there's a small, growing bean of panic lodged in my throat, and it's nourished by the fear that love doesn't come with any guarantees and I could just as easily lose my glorious new boyfriend (in which case, do I lose my best friend too?). Our relationship has—apart from said botch-up—been seamless and wonderful, so I'm hoping and praying that any changes are for the better and don't muck things up. Oh, my jangling nerves are making it difficult to hear myself think.

Toby answers my knock and looks golden and

gorgeous with his thick, blond, stand-up hair and bright blue eyes. "Ella!" he grins.

"Toby!" I grin. "Er . . ."

"So are you going to come in or what?" he continues grinning and takes one step backward.

"Uh, yah, 'course I am," I twitter breathlessly, but attempt to sound flippant. It's this initial breaking-the-ice greeting thing we haven't quite got choreographed just yet. I step toward the radiator-warm belly of the house and glance up at Toby as I pass by him. His face looks calm but his hands are twitchy and his smile hasn't budged. Suddenly and without warning he dips his head in my direction. I'm a little slow to respond so he quickly pulls back just as I push my chin forward to receive his kiss but then rapidly retract it for fear of looking stupid. Then we simultaneously move our heads toward each other and knock foreheads.

Very cool. We both chortle and grimace and try again. It's second-time-lucky and as our mouths touch, our hello-kiss is brief but sweet and gentle. Our lips fit together perfectly and even our noses manage to settle neatly side by side without crashing. We were custom-made for each other.

Just then Toby's spiteful sister, Daftcow Melanie, slithers from the shadows. Lurking quietly in the shadows or basking in the spotlight, Melanie is anything but predictable and usually only sees people in terms of how they can or cannot benefit her world. And if you have no direct benefit then your purpose is to serve as the butt of her jokes. To her I am a butt.

"Oooh la la," she cackles wickedly, like our innocent kiss has a PG-rating or something. "Did I just catch Toby and Ella *snogging*!?" She wraps her shrill observation up in puckered lips and finishes it off with a long, spaghetti-sauce-slurping sound.

"Uh, whatever, Mel," Toby huffs and motions me to the kitchen with his eyeballs. We're like that, Toby and me; we can communicate with our eyeballs. I follow obediently and try to ignore Daftcow who is swaggering behind us with a know-it-all glide in her stride.

"So, how long have you two been a sucky-face couple, then?" she caws, quite obviously relishing her nosy-parker discovery.

"Mind your own beeswax, Melanie," Toby orders and flips the kettle on.

"Yeah . . . mind it . . . " I blither dismally,

eager to back my *boyf* up but still a little wary of Melanie's bite. I can see she's going to be a problem sister-in-law.

"Come on, I think it's cute!" she sings. Daftcow seems to have us confused with furry baby bunny rabbits. "Ah, young love," she finally concludes with a dramatic sigh.

"I said, *whatever*, Melanie—now don't you have your own life to get on with?" Toby meets her head-on.

"Oooh, touchy!" she huffs and finally departs from the kitchen with a nose-in-the-air swank. She obviously doesn't have much going on in the dating department or she'd have definitely given us all the gruesome details.

"What is she like!" I plug the silence and pseudo-fume, like I actually had something to do with that exchange instead of just trailing Toby mindlessly.

Toby abandons the tea assembly and turns to wrap his arms all the way around me. "Forget about her and tell me how *you* are, Ella Mental." He smiles down at me. My heart, along with the rest of my internal organs, does a simultaneous triple somersault.

"Just fine," I gulp deliriously.

"It's nice to see you." His eyes are twinkling mischievously; he can see how nervous I am. There's not much I can hide from Toby.

"And you," I blither stupidly, like I'm having high tea with the Queen. If I'm going to act differently, things are going to be different, I lecture myself. This is good old poo-nappy Toby; I must stop feeling so awkward! "I mean, nice to see you too, Toby Sinclair," I grin and tuck my arms around his waist. There, that's better. This time I reach up to him and, balancing on my tiptoes, settle a light uncomplicated kiss on his lips.

The sound of footsteps stomping down the stairs separates us instantly. "I'm off to see your grandparents!" Mrs. T can be heard yelling from the direction of the living room. "I'll be back in a few hours!"

"Okay, see you later then," Toby replies, giving me a sheepish smirk. Recipe for a tricky situation: take teen romance, add parents, and mix thoroughly.

I'm not sure if Mrs. T even knows that I'm here, but I shout a good-bye just in case. Now that I'm Toby's girlfriend it's very important that I stay on her good side. "How is your mum coping?" I ask Toby, and then straightaway wish I hadn't. Stupid girl! Just as we're getting cozy I go and remind Toby that his traitor dad has set up house with the bleached non-Mrs. T woman.

"She's fine," he replies. "I think she's actually relieved that it's all finally out in the open."

"I can understand that." I nod. "And how are you feeling?" I just don't seem to know when to stop; the wire connecting my mouth to my brain seems to have come loose.

"Okay, I guess. My dad keeps phoning. Mel speaks to him but I've got nothing to say to him yet. Nothing nice, anyway."

"I can understand that, uh, too," I blither. Forget about the loose wire; I have one brain cell and it's taken the day off anyway. The ticking of the grandfather clock in the hallway suddenly seems louder. I don't think Toby wants to discuss his dad any further. Tick tock. Time to change the subject. "You'll never believe what the parental units have come up with this time," I charge ahead. "They've ordered Anna and me to find part-time jobs to earn our own pocket money. And I think they really mean it. Talk about Dullsville!" Of course I can't tell Toby that I'm really against the idea because it'll take me away from him; that'll definitely sound more desperate dolt than liberated lady.

"So what are you going to do then?" he asks.

"I dunno." I sigh. "Poke myself in the eye with a fork maybe?"

Toby gives my suggestion a few moments of thoughtful consideration before responding. "Nah, I don't think you're the street theatre type." He grins. "And there's not much money in it either. Hey, soccer season is winding down and I could also do with some extra cash. How about we find something together?"

"Really?" I squeal loudly. So much for liberated lady then. "I mean, that's a good idea. Do you have anything particular in mind?"

"Mmmm," Toby muses. "We're not quite sixteen yet so that might limit us a little, and I don't much fancy an early morning paper route. But we're both keen on animals, right?" I nod my head madly. "And neither of us is scared of dogs, right?" I shake my head madly. "So how about we set up our own dog-walking business? We could print flyers advertising our services and pop them into Dunton's postboxes. I reckon we could charge at least five quid per dog per hour, and we can pretty much choose our own hours. What do you think?"

I think I'll even clean up soggy dog droppings

while poking myself in the eye with a fork if it means I can be with Toby, and I nod my head madly for the second time in as many minutes. My brain is starting to rattle.

Chapter 3
Lessons in Love

There are now only fifteen days left until Valentine's Day and not only do I not have a card or a collage for Toby, but I still have absolutely zero clue what I'm going to wear. And this is our first Valentine's date, so I've got to look better than great. *CosmoGIRL!* says that this season's big fashion statement is vintage, and the only vintage person I know is my mother—who is a serial hoarder, so there's a good chance she might have something that's so old-fashioned, it's *back in* fashion, hidden somewhere in her cupboard.

It's Sunday morning and both parental units have already left to go to wherever it is units go on Sunday mornings, which gives me the time and the opportunity to have a scout about without letting another soul in on my plan. Today was made to order and I leap from my cozy cocoon and spear the fluffy turquoise dressing gown hanging from its hook on the back of my bedroom door. It may be eight degrees outside, but Dad doesn't like the central heating on for more than a few hours at a time. He says it's not good for us, but I think he really means it's really bad for his pocket.

I emerge from my room and notice that my troublesome twin's bedroom door is still closed, but that could mean anything—Anna never leaves her door open. I glance at my wristwatch. It's almost ten. Anna's definitely still asleep in her bed. I head in the direction of the units' bedroom at the end of the hall and poke my head through the door but make the rest of me wait outside. I must be absolutely certain that both units are out first. Their bedroom is neat and quiet and definitely unit-*less*, so I let the rest of me in and shuffle over to the long, white built-in cupboard that spans the length of one side of the room. The first door reveals Dad's clothes. The second one is hung with various dangling coats. The third has shelves packed with shoe boxes, bags, and cardboard cartons, and I expect that what I'm looking for might possibly be found amongst this lot, but I check the fourth and final door just in case. Just as I thought: not-so-retro motherly clothes.

I return to the shelves and scrape my early morning eyes across the boxes and bags, trying to guess which one might possibly contain fabulous vintage threads that will make me look super-cool. It could be any single one of them. What I'd give for a cup of tea, but the units won't stay away forever so I decide to start at the lowest shelf and work my way up.

The front of the bottom shelf is almost completely taken with a stack of faded *Vogue* magazines that date back to the 1970s. Who knew they had magazines in those days? The model on the cover of the top magazine has the sort of big bouffant hair you could easily mistake for a tea cozy (or maybe I'm still thinking of that cuppa?), and her eye makeup is heavy and dark and fanned by eyelashes that are as long as a cow's (not Daftcow Melanie, mind you—I mean the type you milk). You could take off with those eyelashes if you're not careful, I chuckle.

I pat the space behind the prehistoric *Vogues* with my fingertips, expecting it to be empty, but come across what feels like a pile of paperbacks instead. And although I know full well that vintage fashion feels nothing like paperbacks, I'm in poking-about mode and can't resist mindlessly extracting a few copies from out of the darkness anyway. The books are soft and brown with edges that curl up like Aladdin's shoes. They smell old too, and have titles like *Wings of Desire* and *Flames of Passion* and *Race for Love* with the words *Hearts and Flowers* centered in small curly print above each one.

I notice that each cover is illustrated with a man, a woman, and something in the background. And they've either used the same overworked artist for every book, or everyone's related—because they all look the same. All the women have large melon-breasticles, heart lips, long, wispy hair, and a thing for clingy clothes. All the blokes are tall and knotty with muscles and have Ken-doll square jaws and thick, wavy hair. The only significant difference between each cover is the background, which just might have something to do with the book's title. *Wings of Desire* has a small airplane that's tilted in a climbing position, and the tall, muscled bloke also happens to be wearing a pilot's uniform, so no prizes for guessing what that one's about. The *Flames of Passion* bloke is covered in black grime and seems to be wearing fireman's pants and boots. There's also a burning building in the background. Directly below the title *Race for Love* is a chestnut racehorse that's flat and stretched out in a gallop, although the cover bloke is far too brawny to be a jockey. He's dressed in a sharp suit, so maybe he's a gambler or he owns the horse or it's his day off. Or something.

With dwindling interest and fashion on my mind I toss the books to the carpet, but the one on top—*Race for Love*, springs open on page forty-two. I can't help it; I'm too nosy not to notice. I retrieve the paperback and start reading. . . .

"Tell me you feel it too, Taylor," Sven growled hoarsely, breathing in her musky scent. "I don't believe you're willing to spend the rest of your life not knowing, not knowing what it might be like . . . what we might be like!" He gazed deeply into her shimmering hazel eyes and lovingly tucked an escaped tendril of long dark hair behind her delicately shaped ear.

"I can't Sven, I just can't," Taylor stammered. She must think about Hugh and forget all about Sven and how he makes her feel like a real woman. She breathed deeply to steady herself and her soft, full breasts rose and fell. Ignoring her pleas,

Sven circled her small waist with his large masculine hands. His fingertips brushed the warm flesh of her flat belly.

"I love you, Taylor," Sven whispered. He covered her mouth with his lips. Her resistance gave way and he explored her mouth and tasted her sweetness.

Ah! I snap the book shut and squeeze the edges tightly closed, as if trying to contain Sven and Taylor and their forbidden hanky panky inside the pages. My eyes are as big and round as tennis balls and jump off the page and bounce around the room to make sure that nobody has caught me reading this . . . this er, rather interesting piece of literature. They don't stock any of this "Hearts and Flowers" business in the Dunton school library, that's for certain. Or maybe I just landed on a particularly saucy book, and the rest of them are straightforward and quite wholesome. I reach for *Wings of Desire* and let it fall open on the carpet. These books have a mind of their own! I begin reading at page fifty-three. . . .

Rick found her in the first-class cabin gathering up her belongings, ready to disembark the deserted plane. "Where do you think you're going?" he shouted angrily. His starched captain's uniform gleamed in the early morning light.

"What do you mean?" Misty replied, surprised by his sudden appearance.

"You know exactly what I mean!" Rick growled and covered the space between them in three strides of his long lithe legs. "No more games," he added, moving up close to her and breathing in her captivating and seductive perfume. "I know you love and want me just as much as I love and want you!" He silenced her with his open mouth. . . .

Mother! It's a miracle the woman only has two kids (and we are twins, you know—two birds and one stone and all of that). Speaking of which, I wonder if Dad knows about these "Hearts and Flowers" books? Ugh! Now there's a thought I wished I hadn't had.

"Now what?" I mutter quietly to myself and stare at *Wings of Desire* and *Race for Love* and poor, confused Taylor and passionate Rick and Sven who all quite obviously have so much to teach me. My conscience is telling me to do one thing but my teenage heart and hormones are demanding that I do quite another. I slide a hand back into the darkness, past Miss *Vogue* and her tea-cozy head, and feel around for more of the devilish paperbacks. There are at least another two, three . . . six, seven . . . ten or so. *My mother has no shame!* Still, it's somehow reassuring to know that she is vaguely human and not the holy, super-organized, no-nonsense lawmaker she always seems to be. "So there's a bit of motor in her rotor after all," I chuckle to myself. Conveniently forgetting my scratchy conscience, I grab the three "Hearts and Flowers" novels and scoot from the units' bedroom as fast as my slippers and gown will take me. I can't risk borrowing them all in one go!

Chapter 4

Strength in Numbers

The only bad thing about a weekend is that it's chased by a Monday, which begins a week of early mornings, school, and—in winter—very short days. The afternoon is barely three and a half hours old and we've only just escaped the classroom, but already the daylight is dipping and giving in to dusk. The winter months have reduced the once ripe and heavy trees and shrubs of Dunton to skinny skeleton branches that are as hard and jagged as lightning bolts, and the sky above is opaque and vaporous—like somebody in heaven left the freezer door open or something. I'm busy concentrating on hopping from one foot to the other, trying to keep my body temperature from dropping below zero and peering through the foggy condensation billowing from my lips. Forget dog-walking, I'd do well as a Puff the Magic Dragon impersonator.

"You need thick woolly tights." Frannie states the obvious and burrows her hands deeper into the padded pockets of her jacket while hunching her shoulders around her ears.

"I need to be home and in my bed," I reply curtly. My mood is as chilly as the winter air. Fran, Pearl, and I have been standing outside the school gates waiting for Toby and Tom-Tom for the past fifteen minutes, and my patience is disappearing along with the feeling in my toes. I do not like the cold one bit.

"I'm dying for a fag!" Pearl bleats wistfully.

"Yup, that's true," I agree, not missing a single opportunity to soapbox my cigarette-equals-cancer-stick viewpoint.

"I bet you could have a fag right here and nobody would even notice," Fran grins, glancing around at all the other kids heading for home, the bus, or toasty parent-cars. "Look," she demonstrates, puffing into the icy air, "that could easily be smoke—who would know the difference?"

"Don't you go encouraging her," I scowl at Fran.

"You can be such a geriatric sometimes, Ella!" Pearl glares at me and shakes her head impatiently.

"And you can be so juvenile," I volley. We've all been best mates since primary school so we're allowed to be touchy or bossy or impatient with one another sometimes.

Since shifting up to Year 11 we share certain

classes some of the time, but even though we're not together every minute of the day we always hang out during break and still spend practically every spare moment together. We balance one another out nicely; we're like our own little second family. Just then, Toby and Tom-Tom emerge from the uniformed crowd and cozily slip in between us girls to scrounge off our body heat.

"Where have you boys been?" Frannie asks. "Ella's been whining for the last ten minutes!"

"Well, we have been hanging about in the cold waiting for you blokes and I have a bladder as full as a freaking fish tank," I gripe. It's really not my fault.

Toby looks at me thoughtfully, like I'm a riddle he's trying to solve. "How nice for you, Ella," he says slowly, smiling at me strangely.

"Yeah well . . . that's how it is," I sulk, although I don't suppose that the "freaking fish tank" analogy was very ladylike or alluring. I somehow can't imagine "Hearts and Flowers" Misty updating Rick on the status of her bladder.

"Are we off then?" Pearl asks impatiently, no doubt still hankering after her coffin-nail fags.

"Yeah, let's move it," Tom-Tom orders, and takes the lead.

Nobody says another word and we all automatically fall in with the tall boy with curly black hair setting the pace. Our friend has become noticably more self-assured and outspoken since the terrifying bullying ordeal he suffered at the hands of John Bennie and his thugs in the basement of the boiler room not so long ago, and each one of us is secretly in awe of this brand-new confident Tom Toisin who seems to have taken over from the small stuttering boy who earned himself the nickname Tom-Tom all those years ago. He looks liberated, like he's already confronted his worst demons and no longer fears fear in any way. But we'll always call him Tom-Tom. We could never forget that small stuttering boy who helped build this brave young man up.

As Toby and I move in beside each other I'm suddenly grateful for the sharp cold that's insisting we walk with our hands submerged deep in our pockets. It's not that I don't want to hold Toby's hand, but we're still at that clumsy stage. And not only is it awkward deciding who should make the first move, but it still feels seriously weird holding hands in front of our mates who I just know will quickly swivel their eyeballs sideways in our direction (but of course pretend not to). Thank goodness we have Tom-Tom's chattering to divert us away from any uncomfortable moments.

He's been working late into the night to create a website he's called Pinboard Psychology for Teens, and he's asked us to take a look at it and offer our opinions. He talks as we walk and describes how he's designed the website specifically for teenagers, with the purpose of creating a meeting place where young people can communicate openly and post messages about anything and everything. Whether they have a problem that needs answering, a concern that needs airing, advice that may prove useful, or a thought that might inspire others—he says that we're all here to help one another. So Pinboard Psychology for Teens—or PPT, as he's already calling it—is basically a chat room where teenagers can post messages either asking for help or offering advice, and the engine powering the entire concept is that nobody should feel alone because we all need somebody to talk to—somebody who understands what we're feeling. And who better to offer advice and a viewpoint than somebody who is actually going through the same thing, he adds enthusiastically. Not only is this new

Tom-Tom more confident, he's also a lot more talkative! The idea is his and he's built the site—self-taught—from scratch. Something tells me that Tom-Tom is the most likely to succeed out of us all.

By the time we reach the small duplex Tom-Tom shares with his mum and younger brother I'm joined at the knees and toddling along like a penguin. I'm trying to be subtle but as soon as Tom-Tom unlocks the front door I'm the first one through it. I gallop for the urination station at the end of the hallway and lock myself inside. If the cold seat isn't a showstopper then the fact that I can clearly hear Toby and the rest of my mates chattering just a few steps away definitely is, so I inspect the bathroom to take my mind off my stage fright. There's an ornately framed plaque hanging on the back of the door that reads:

If you sprinkle
When you tinkle,
Be a sweetie
And wipe the seatie.

That's what you get for having two sons, Mrs. Toisin, I remark, and suddenly wish I'd checked the seat before sitting down. Everything is silent; my bladder seems to be punishing me for making it wait so long. I'm supposed to head home straight after school and do my homework before I go anywhere, but I am a teenager. That's like ordering me not to get pimples. And besides, the parental units never return home from work before six anyway. It's a very worthwhile risk. The heating is switched on and I run my frosty mitts across the sizzling side of the small radiator attached to the wall, trying to get some feeling back into my fingertips. And it helps, in more ways than one.

By the time I emerge from the urination station, Tom-Tom, Toby, and the girls have the kettle on and PPT up and open on the PC monitor that's resting on the beech-effect computer desk standing neatly in the corner of the floral-splash Toisin living area.

"So has your snarky mood improved then, Ella Mental?" Pearl spies me and yaps irritably. Somebody obviously hasn't ventured outside for their nicotine yet. So winter does have an upside, for Pearl's lungs at least. I don't respond to her jab and take a peek at Tom-Tom's fancy new creation instead. The website looks really slick and funky and very professional indeed. Centred at the top of the homepage are the letters *PPT* enclosed in a black, egg-shaped casing that looks like it's been stamped onto the page. Centered directly below this, in bold, attention-grabbing script, are the words *Pinboard Psychology for Teens* followed by the sentence: "Teens helping teens to help themselves." Tom-Tom is going to make headlines!

"It really looks brilliant," I gush with heartfelt enthusiasm and pat his back affectionately. "Well done!"

Tom-Tom smiles and looks secretly pleased with himself, but attempts to camouflage his pride by immediately launching into a formally guided tour of the site. The homepage includes a short welcome note that pretty much outlines exactly what Tom-Tom explained to us on the way over here—giving visitors an overview of what the site is really about. There's an index to the left of this that offers options like: Read Entry, Make New Entry, and Search Entries. He's also included links to other useful websites such as Alateens, Embarrassing Health Problems, the Eating Disorders Association, Sexwise, and Youth Access.

"So have you had any hits yet?" Toby asks

with sparkly flying-saucer eyes. He's obviously as impressed as I am.

"Well, I secretly posted one myself," Tom-Tom replies sheepishly, and then grins. "Anonymously, of course, you know—just to get the ball rolling."

"Hey, why don't we all post a message," I suggest excitedly, "and soon PPT will be the most popular site on the Internet!" We all nod enthusiastically and Tom-Tom chuckles happily.

"Hey, why don't you also set up a chat room for singles—you know the kind where you list your profile with a photo and stuff, and girls and guys with similar interests chat and get to know each other and stuff?" Pearl uses the word *stuff* when she's excited.

"Can't you get your mind off the opposite sex for one brief moment, Pearl?" Fran chastizes her. "This isn't supposed to be a lonely hearts online dating club."

Pearl's gusto turns bristly. "The thought hadn't even crossed my mind."

Crossed her mind? Pah, the thought sat down, burrowed a small hole, and laid an egg in your head, I think to myself (but don't dare breathe the words out loud). Pearl may be a portable hormone, but I think I've already used up my snotty allowance for the afternoon.

"Sorry, Pearl, but there are loads of those sites out there." Tom-Tom smiles consolingly.

"And I'm sure you have most of them book-marked in your Favorites," Toby joins in with a playful snicker.

"Oh, what would you lot know about it!" Pearl snaps and stomps her way out the back door. "I'm off to have a fag, then."

Chapter 5
Strained Relations

This week has been put to good use. Inspired by Tom-Tom's brilliant website creation, Toby and I have put a lot of time and effort into creating our very own personalized dog-walking flyers, or uh, flyers that advertise our dog-walking services, rather. Toby has a fancy color printer so they're vibrant and eye-catching and should hopefully get our phones ringing any day now. And if the actual dog-walking turns out to be a fraction as much fun as making the flyers then I'm definitely one delirious lady in love. If I'd known that being Toby's girlfriend would be this wonderfully awesome I would have vied for the position a long time ago! Who'd have guessed that something as ordinary as working together on the computer could be so intense and dreamy? I felt like a creature in one of those Discovery Channel nature programs—the ones where they slow everything down and magnify each sight and sound to correspond with what the insect or animal sees and hears. Every one of my senses felt amplified and heightened to the point where even something as simple as my hand brushing against Toby's seemed momentous and felt crackly and hot and rasped loudly like paper tearing in my ear.

We've spent a good part of our Saturday morning hand-delivering our fancy flyers to the post boxes and doorways of Dunton, but it's almost noon, so Toby has swapped me for soccer and left me to wander the road that will join another road that will eventually take me home. I'm *boyf*-less for the rest of the afternoon. Sigh. I pass the edge of the park with the bench and the road that leads to Frannie's house. I haven't been to her house or seen Maria Mendes—her mum—since that fateful day Fran's heart cracked open and all the bad stuff about her Uncle Mannie came seeping out like an oozing infection. I didn't even see Fran for a few weeks after that. She took some time away with her devastated mum and dad and when she came back she looked a little lighter, stronger and a watered down version of angry. She didn't mention Uncle Mannie to me for the first few days—it was almost like nothing terrible had even happened. But then one day she unexpectedly handed me a letter sealed tightly in an envelope. Her face told me exactly what it was about so I carried it home safely and read it in private a hundred times over before finally tearing it into shreds so small not even one single word remained whole or legible. All that was left was a pulpy pile of paper fragments, some of them scribbled with random letters of the alphabet in Frannie's black-ink pen, others empty or edged in loops and lines of disemboweled letters. All the king's horses and all the king's men couldn't have put those shredded tatters back together again. But I remember every single word and the order in which Frannie wrote them like her letter was tattooed on the back of my eyelids.

She said that telling me her secret was both the hardest and, in some strange way, also an easy thing for her to do. She thanked me for listening and for telling her mum. She also thanked me for not judging her. It seems that as we were sitting on the bench talking in the park that day she had decided in her head that my reaction would determine whether or not she would make it through this; she didn't think she could survive me looking at her like she was sick or gross or evil. She said in a way I saved her.

She also mentioned that Mannie is now in

jail and registered on the sex offenders' list as a convicted pedophile. But most importantly of all, she told me that she's started seeing a psychologist who has assured her that the guilt isn't hers any more. Seems it never was. She ended up by asking me to please never ever tell another single soul about any of this. Not Toby, not Anna, not anybody. She said that if I loved her I would keep it a secret forever, and she signed the letter simply with a cross for a kiss.

It used to be that I would stop by Frannie's any old time, but now I'm waiting for an invitation—nothing formal or fancy, just a few small words to let me know that the Mendes family is ready to open the ranks and allow outsiders back in again. And if I'm completely truthful, as much as I adore Fran's warm and wonderful units, I don't know that I'm ready to see them yet either. I'm terrified they're going to want to talk about the day I had no other choice but to sit on the couch in their cozy family room with its wall of sentimental photographs, and tell Maria what Frannie had just told me Uncle Mannie used to do to her when she was a kid and nobody else was about. Adults are like that. They like to talk about things way too much. And mums are usually the worst.

So I keep walking along the road that will take me home to my own parental rule-freak units and quite possibly my toffee-nosed twin too. Throw another family meeting into the mix and we have the makings of a really rubbish Saturday. I heave my second huge sigh of the day.

I'm almost home when Mum clanks past me in the faded-blue Renault she insists on calling Bluebell. She pokes a hand out the half-open window and jiggles her fingers at me as she goes by but doesn't bother stopping. She could have driven past ten minutes ago, I shiver—shifting up a gear to cover the few remaining meters home. This is turning out to be one of those days.

Anna must have been in the car with Mum because by the time I reach home, the pair of them are still fussing and faffing about with various shopping bags in the driveway.

"Thanks for the lift," I grumble, simply for the sake of it.

"Oh please, Ella, don't be silly!" Mum clucks as she fiddles with her oversized bunch of keys. Anna's coat is unbuttoned and I can see that she's wearing a denim skirt with a fancy-shmancy top I don't believe I've ever seen before. I'm almost sure I haven't seen that skirt either, come to think of it. The suede boots are familiar, but that's about it. She's also got her hair all done up and is wearing enough makeup to get arrested, even though we're supposedly only allowed to use lipstick and mascara. So this is what goes on when my back is turned and I'm out trying to earn an honest wage!

"Oi, what's going on here?" I bleat with my forehead furrowed in a frown. "Have you just been shopping for new clothes? And what's with the face paint?"

"Oh, do calm down, Ella," Mum groans tiredly as she closes Bluebell's door with her bottom and shuffles toward the front door of our house. Anna, who is now standing behind Mum, suddenly pulls her coat open with a flourish and begins wiggling her new denim hips brazenly and bouncing her eyebrows at me. The smug, tonsil-exposing smirk stretched across her face says it all and I've a good mind to give her a finger-flick between the eyes (she really hates that and deserves it too). But Mum was the leader of this sneaky, Saturday-morning shopping expedition so I decide to focus my outrage on her instead.

"They are new clothes!" I protest loudly. And I know, because I'd have borrowed that skirt a long time ago. "Would you mind telling me just what is going on here?" Mum ignores me and heads indoors. "No thanks, I didn't want to come shopping," I continue, following her closely. "I don't need new clothes. I'll just make do with the kitchen rag when you're done with it, thank you very much." I'm having a Cinderella moment. Just as I'm getting into the full swing of my victim routine Mum all of a sudden swivels to face me.

"Would you put a sock in it, Ella!" she barks, and exhales noisily, as if drawing on her final reserve of strength. "I did try calling you on your mobile before we left—I let it ring all the way to voicemail, and you know your father's rule about being able to reach you at all times. This morning Anna auditioned to be the new face of Marks & Spencer. Your Aunty Chloe set it up, she's now second-in-charge of their marketing department and she pulled a few strings. Anna had to show up for a test shoot, so she needed something nice to wear and had her makeup done for free at the Revlon counter at Boots. So it's your own fault you missed it all, young lady, not mine."

Ah right. I have a vague memory of a call from home. I thought it was one of the units calling about an outstanding chore, so I shoved my phone under Mrs. T's sofa cushions until it went quiet.

But I've still got plenty of other things to protest about—I just don't know where to begin, and I stand there, silently irked, with my jaws moving up and down like I'm bobbing for apples instead. First and foremost in a very long list: even though I'd rather floss with razor wire than be the new face of Marks & Spencer, everybody seems to be overlooking one very significant fact here—that Anna and I are T-W-I-N-S! Dictionary definition: the exact counterpart of a person or thing! So would somebody please tell me why neither Mum nor Aunt Chloe had bothered to ask me if I'd like to audition too? Why don't they just tattoo the words *the ugly one* on my forehead and be done with it? And secondly, if Anna wants to be a model and therefore gets new clothes, does that mean that because I'm going to be a dog-walker that I get a dog? Because I'd very much like a puppy, thank you very much. And here's a thought: Why are the units helping Anna with her part-time job and yet nobody has even offered me so much as a refreshing cup of tea to help me along with mine? And another thing: Should we really be encouraging

Anna? Isn't she full of herself enough already? But instead of saying any one of these things out loud, all I do is stand there sputtering and fizzing in frustration while Mum stares at me hand-on-hip expectantly.

"Right then," she finally sighs, evidently losing interest in my stammering and shifting her focus to the kitchen.

"But it's not fair!" I manage to wail after her pitifully.

"What's not fair?" Dad appears from nowhere and butts in.

"Life . . ." I mumble miserably but don't dish out any details. Like he would really care.

"It's been a week since our last family meeting, Ella." He disregards my gloominess and sets off in a commanding tone, "What's the status on your part-time job hunt then?"

Could this be the most irritating family in the whole entire galaxy? I wonder as I yank my last dog-walking flyer from my pocket, shove it at Dad, and blaze a trail up the stairs to my bedroom instead. What a bunch of Anna-lovers!

Chapter 6
Dogwalks and Catwalks

The glorious event that is Valentine's Day falls on a miserable Monday so my mates and I have taken the liberty of moving it three days forward to tomorrow, which is a fab Friday. And even though my romantic evening with Toby really involves a triple date to the movies with Pearl and her new boyfriend, Archie, and Fran and Tom-Tom (who definitely aren't a couple but will get a giggle out of pretending to be), I'm nevertheless looking forward to celebrating the occasion. I'll still be buying Valentine's cards, only this year they won't be anonymous and I won't be posting them to myself. Mrs. Bennett-from-the-post-office will just have to get her laughs some other way this Valentine's.

With the collage idea officially tossed in the bin (way too childish!), I've decided to write Toby a romantic poem, which is why I've got my nose tucked firmly in between the pages of *Flames of Passion.* I'm looking to Tucker and April for romantic inspiration this time. I used to get most of my tips from *CosmoGIRL!* but these days "Hearts and Flowers" is becoming my one-stop shop for just about everything love-related. I wonder if the editor of *CG!* has read *Flames of Passion*?

Tucker's love for April was as scorching as the fire he'd just extinguished. Beads of sweat snaked between his heaving abs, but he was oblivious to his exhaustion. He could only think about the breathtaking blonde standing nearby wearing Lycra shorts and a cropped top. The fire must have interrupted her workout.

Tucker walked over and whispered: "You're as beautiful as a full moon on a clear night." He touched her arm; her skin felt smooth and hotter than the steamy summer air around them. He wished they were alone.

"And you're as sweet as a honeysuckle," she purred. Tucker's closeness was making her giddy, or maybe it was the heat—but either way, April was finding him hard to resist. She knew that once he kissed her she would be lost, but she no longer cared. She no longer cared that he was grimy or spelled trouble with a capital T. The last thing she needed right now was to fall for this handsome, flirty firefighter, but as he moved his lips along her ear—planting small delicate kisses along the way—her breath subconsciously caught on his name. It was too late; she had fallen in love. . . .

I read to the end of the chapter and close my eyes and the book, feeling breathless and flushed. I probably shouldn't, but I can't help wondering if Toby feels the same way about me. Although April does prance about in pretty Lycra outfits while I'm currently wearing my tatty *Star Trek* flannel PJs. We really do present two very different images and mine probably needs a buff up, which might just be my belated New Year's resolution.

While *Flames of Passion* has left me with some interesting fodder for thought, what it hasn't done is help to resolve my Valentine's gift dilemma. I'm contemplating my alternatives when I suddenly hear my name being called from out of nowhere. I should have known my starchy conscience would make an appearance at some point. Crumbs and freaking crikey—I am almost sixteen years old, and I'm only borrowing the books!

"Ella, are you awake?"

My conscience is not usually this considerate, and although neither is Anna, the voice suddenly sounds suspiciously like hers. I frantically shove *Flames of Passion* underneath my bed and partially emerge from the crumpled mound of my duvet.

"Yuh, what?" I mumble. The door clicks, opens, shuts, and suddenly Anna is looking down at me. Some things never change.

"It's not even eight o'clock, what are you doing in bed?" she demands.

"What's it to you?" I grumble, sandwiching my fiery cheeks between the duvet and my pillow. I'm not very good at keeping secrets like this from my twin and I can feel *Flames of Passion* burning a hole all the way through my bed's base and mattress.

"Guess what?" Anna gasps, ignoring my guilty tone. She never did care why I was in bed in the first place, anyway. "Aunt Chloe just called Mum—they loved me. I am officially the new face of Marks & Spencer."

Of course you are, I want to humph but know full well that it will sound spiteful. I know this because I'm feeling spiteful; I'm still severely irked that I wasn't even considered for the job. I haven't forgotten about the twin thing, even if everybody else has. And even though I know it's not fair to take this out on Anna, sometimes you just can't help the way you feel. The best you can do is swallow it down and try to avoid doing or saying anything you might regret later, when those irky feelings have long gone. It's called considering the consequences of your actions, and it's seriously useful Good Sense logic.

"That's cool, Anna," I say instead, trying to scrape together as much zeal as I have inside me. "That's really cool. . . ."

If my enthusiasm sounds forced Anna doesn't seem to notice or care. "Aunt Chloe sent these back to me today," she continues, waving a brown envelope at me. "Here—take a look!" She's hopping about from one foot to the other like she's performing a highland jig and it takes me three grabby attempts before I finally manage to pull the envelope from her white-knuckled grip. Inside is a batch of glossy color photographs of Anna—offset by an eggshell studio background—sitting and standing and pouting and posing in various positions. I recognize the makeup, the hair and the outfit from Sneaky Saturday.

I sift through the photos, inspecting each one with dutiful interest. Anna looks strikingly pretty and rather glam. She definitely has a presence about her (Pearl calls it a *pretense*, but perhaps she's just jealous). Anna never slouches and always keeps her spine straight, her shoulders back, and her chin up. She meets and holds people with her eyes, and it's apparent that she has a similar knack with the camera. Perhaps she's right; she just might have what it takes to be a model. I, for one, would now definitely consider stopping off at Marks & Spencer.

Anna's hair is longer and one shade closer to blonde than mine, and she's plucked and polished in all the places I am not. I'm more of a first-thing-in-the-morning version of my sister, except I don't usually improve as the day goes on. I've got the disheveled, washed-out quirky thing going on while Anna is usually groomed, poised, and radiant. Granted, she spends more time primping than I do, but she sparkles from the inside out. She radiates confidence, and her attitude is catching. You'd only feel silly questioning or rallying against the strength of the force that is Anna's self-belief.

"So?" she gushes, unable to hold back her enthusiasm any longer.

"These really are great!" I smile up at her. And I mean it. They really are. "You look fab and Marks & Sparks is lucky to have you."

She shares my smile. "Yes, they are, aren't they." This may sound giant-headed, but that's just Anna calling it as she sees it.

"Best mugshots I've ever seen," I grin broadly, giving her a jokey wink.

"I think you'll find they're called *head* shots, Ella," she replies carefully, like I'm dim-witted but essentially harmless so she'll let it pass.

"Toby and I are setting up our own dog-walking service," I offer, fairly confident that she'd never have got around to asking. "We've printed flyers and everything."

"Er, that's . . . cool," Anna burbles and suddenly looks uncharacteristically awkward. She doesn't think it's cool at all and really pities me. I hadn't given it much thought up until now, but suddenly I'm feeling a little sorry for me too. It's so freaking typical: Anna becomes a paid model and I take up dog-walking. Paid dog-walking hopefully, but so double-freaking what? The universe is vicious and cruel.

"Well . . . Toby and I are also going on a Valentine's date tomorrow night," I blither, squaring my shoulders. I don't mention that it's actually a triple date with our mates of course.

"Hey, that's brilliant!" Anna gushes with the sort of over-the-top enthusiasm that's probably better suited to a Nobel Peace Prize recipient or something. "I could do your nails for you, if you like? I have a spare set of falsies."

I'm just about to decline (I don't usually do falsie-anything), but situations have changed drastically. I'm Toby's girlfriend now, and it's high time I started making more of an effort with my appearance. My bruised-black thumbnail is only just beginning to fade after being slammed in Bluebell's door two weeks ago and the three adjacent nails are still stained a faint yellow from when I spilled antiseptic while attending to my injured thumb. Attractive, I think not. "Uh, okay, sure," I nervously give in.

Chapter 7
Fright Night

"We're almost done . . ." Anna murmurs to no one in particular. Her tongue is curling up and out of her mouth and almost touching her nose, and at a quick glance it looks like her top lip is a plump, veiny slug. "Right, *now* you can look!" she declares with a flourish.

Not only have I let Anna glue bits of acrylic to my fingertips, but I've let her do my hair and apply mascara and lipstick to my face too. She's also insisted on choosing a "very special outfit" for me, and I will now be stepping out in a cream skirt with a chocolate frilly hem, a matching cashmere polo neck and her suede boots. And I'm only going to the movies with my mates.

It's my own fault; I haven't had the courage to tell Anna that tonight really involves six people and a very dark cinema. She seems so happy for me, like I finally have some joy in my life and she's determined to make it memorable. Of course Anna doesn't mind that she's Valentine-*less* one bit. She's just spent the last twenty minutes explaining to me that she's a single career girl now and romance would only fuss with her future. So I've become her pet project, a channel for all her pent-up affection.

I swivel in my desk chair to face the square mirror that's propped up against my school textbooks. The first thing I notice is my hair. Anna wasn't wrong about the "wild look" (which required lashings of mousse and me hanging upside down with a hair dryer pressed against my head). I certainly look like I've just emerged from some far-flung jungle where I very well might have been living remotely like a wild madwoman for some time. I don't know if this is the sort of wild Anna had in mind, but that's definitely the look we have going on here.

I study my lips in the mirror and then pluck the tube of lipstick from Anna's grip. It's called "Glittergirl Pink" and it's long-lasting. Of course it is. You could land an airplane in the dark with my lips. The only bit of me that doesn't leave me nauseous are my eyelashes. The mascara job is a little heavy but sort of okay. At least my eyelids will get a workout. What an evening this is going to be.

"Come on, time to get dressed!" Anna grins

excitedly. She's mistaken my stumped suffering for gobsmacked glee. How do I tell her that it's not that sort of evening (that it's Valentine's, not *Halloween*)? I peek at the skirt with the dark frilly hem lying in wait on the bed for me. A triple date to the movies is hardly even a date at all! I have to come clean; it's the only sensible plan of action.

"Ella?"

"Uh huh?" I croak and slowly turn to face Anna with eyes that are wide and glassy with dread.

"I want you to know that I think it's sooooo super-amazing that you and Toby are together. I always knew that you were made for each other, it was written in the stars. And he obviously loves you a lot if he's arranged this special evening for the two of you. You look beautiful! I hope you have a great time," she concludes and folds me in a hug. In Anna's eyes I've redeemed my dog-walking self by having this fabulous love life. And as she stands there glowing proudly at me all I can do is smile limply and drag myself toward the frilly skirt and boots. I now desperately need a plan B.

Toby usually meets me on the corner outside

our house (I like to keep him far from the units) and my spur-of-the-moment emergency plan B is to get there before him and do what I can to quickly tame my head and my lips. So I dress in double-quick time, squeeze Anna, and finally charge downstairs without falling off the boots. I've already cleared my plans with the units and simply holler "I'm off!" as I pass them on my way to the front door, which all of a sudden ding-dongs just as I'm about to reach for the handle.

I skim the surface of my brain, desperately and frantically trying to think of who else could possibly be standing on the other side of the door. Although I don't know why I bother. Of course it's Toby. And even though I know that he's just trying to be a five-star boyfriend, I have an instant urge to pinch him. But that won't help the situation, so I lick both palms and frantically begin wiping them on my hair over and over, like a cat grooming itself.

Ding-dong.

I want to shout out, "I've got it!" but then Toby will know that I'm standing on the other side of the door—just inches away from him, so I hobble over to the units who are still watching telly, give them a wordless grin and a thumbs-up and hobble back to the door to suck on my lips.

Silence. Ding-dong.

"Ella?" Mum calls from the living room.

It's now or never. I climb into the longest coat on the rack, switch off the outside light, open the door a crack and squeeze through it.

"Hey, Tobes." I grimace and give the full moon a filthy look.

"Hey, Ellie." He's staring at my head. "You look uh…nice."

"Ah yeah, whatever." I feel seriously silly and quickly toddle along the path with my head down. Not only do I want to escape from our house, which is lit up like Piccadilly Circus, but I'm terrified Toby will try and kiss me on the doorstep. And there's no doubt in my mind that some member of my meddling family will be pressing their curious beak against a window pane to see what we're up to.

Toby jogs to catch me up and we walk in silence for a bit. "Are you okay?" he finally asks.

I slow my pace but still avoid his eye. "Course I am," I reply brightly. I'm starting to feel a little better now that my house, the Addams family, and the lights have faded into the background. I even manage a smile.

"That's better!" he cheers and scoops my hand up in his. We continue walking and making small talk until the Friday night colors and sounds of Dunton's High Street creep into focus.

"Before we meet up with that lot I want to give you something," Toby says, tugging me to a standstill and suddenly looking pink and shy. He dips his hand into his coat pocket and offers up a small, shiny-foil carrier bag with matching cord handles. His face is stretched with a nervous grin that's drained the blood from his lips.

I accept the bag and scoop out its insides. My first ever Valentine's gift (from somebody else) is a soft, brown teddy bear with a sherbet-pink heart embroidered on its chest. There's also a card and as I gracelessly grapple to open the envelope with my falsies my brain gnaws on two thoughts. The first is that it's taking me forever to get this wretched envelope open, and the second is that Toby is noticably staring at the ridiculous bits of plastic glued to my fingertips. And he obviously thinks they're horrible, because he's keeping dead quiet about them.

In utter desperation I eventually slash the envelope open with my acrylic claws. Finally they're good for something! The cover of the card is illustrated with a cartoon of a boy and girl sitting on a hilltop underneath a giant light bulb that's hanging down from the heavens. I open the card. It says: *You light up my life* in bright yellow print. Below this, written in Toby's unmistakable blue-ink capitals, it reads:

> DEAR ELLA,
> HAPPY VALENTINE'S.
> TOBY X

Not one mention of love then, but I'll take what I can get.

"It's beautiful, thank you," I say and burrow inside my own coat pocket for the small parcel wrapped in chubby cherubs. "This is for you." I've taken the safe yet bland route and instead of a romantic poem or a baby-photo collage, Toby's Valentine's gift consists of a card and a pair of Manchester United socks. They're the ones with side air vents, so your feet don't sweat or smell.

I subconsciously resume sucking my glitter lips while I watch him read his card. On the cover—surrounded by candy-colored hearts—are printed the words *Do you know what I like about you?* The answer, printed on the inside, is:

Everything! Not very original or *Romeo and Juliet*, but I ran out of time. Still, I have made some attempt to be creative and scribbled a few sentences describing what our relationship means to me inside the card. Er, a few sentences...four paragraphs, what's the difference? Toby's cheeks have suddenly caught alight.

"I'll save that for later, huh?" He grins nervously. "Thanks, Ellie."

"You're welcome," I mumble. One paragraph probably would have done it.

Toby takes a step forward, circles me with his arms and stoops to settle his lips on my own. I'd like to lose myself in the Valentine moment but this kiss is bound to involve tongues so I need to concentrate; coordinating all those teeth and two noses requires skill and agility, even when you're custom-made for each other.

As I stand there with my chin up, nestled in his strong arms, I still can't believe that somebody as beautiful and funny and wonderful as Toby Sinclair would choose me for his girlfriend. Tonight he smells like the ocean and as I hold on tightly and dissolve into our kiss I can't help noticing that his waist is taut and his stomach ridged with muscles. This gets me thinking: April wouldn't just stand there, would she? She'd run her hands through his hair and whisper his name softly. Tucker's name, that is, not Toby's. Perhaps I also need to be more romantic. So reeling in my courage I tentatively lift my right hand from Toby's waist and move it up to his head, where I then proceed to run my fingers through his lovely blond hair.

If I'm entirely honest, this new found lovey-dovey stuff is not coming naturally to me, but then perhaps being romantic is like eating spaghetti and requires technique and practice.

If Toby's enjoying the whole fingers-through-the-hair experience he's not letting on either, and after a while our kissing slows and we finally break for air. As I take a step backward, I can't help noticing the tiny crease that's settled between his eyes. It's so tiny, in fact, that anybody else might not even have noticed it. But I have, and if I didn't know any better I might think that he was looking bewildered and just a little bit anxious.

"Uh, shall we get going?" he finally asks, glancing in the direction of the cinema. And that's when I see it. There, caught up in Toby's hair like a dangling fish scale, is one of my falsies!

Chapter 8
Talking Heads

From where I'm sitting I can clearly make out the gaggle of giggling young children waddling over to the old Catholic Church for Sunday school, while on my right a group of skater boys with scruffy heads dressed in baggy denim and plump trainers work their skateboards in the park's parking lot. They're the reason few cars ever park here; runaway skateboards leave impressive dents. Not that we have to worry. Dunton is a small village and we walk just about everywhere, which is just as well—considering that we don't have cars or even drive.

The sun may be visible and the winter chill slowly thawing out, but I'm still using the weather as an excuse to cuddle up closer to Toby. Pearl is rocking on her butt cheeks with her knees up, gibbering on about poor Archie, who we all think is cool but Pearl thinks not.

"I mean, what kind of bloke doesn't even kiss you on Valentine's?" She tut-tuts.

"Well, you have only just met," Frannie speaks out (the rest of us have the sense not to), "and we were all there too, remember. What were you expecting from the guy?"

"Oh bollocks, that's why you go to movies in the first place." Pearl educates the rest of us. "Whatcha think they turn the lights out for, huh? No, the problem with Archie is he's immature. I need an older man for sure."

I slip Toby a secret smile. He appears equally amused; Pearl and her hormones definitely have some entertainment value. We may have celebrated Valentine's Day on Friday, but romance is definitely still floating about in the air and Toby and I are feeling seriously lovey-dovey. Miss Cotton, our social studies teacher, says that Valentine's is nothing more than a pointless money-making racket, but the fact that she has a moustache a walrus would be proud of might have something to do with this. Personally, I think that any occasion that encourages love and helps us to forget about all the ugliness in the world—even if just for one day (or a weekend, in our case)—can't be bad. I sidle up a few millimeters closer to Toby and hook my pinkie with his. Being loved-up rules!

"I saw that look, Ella Mental," Pearl suddenly shouts, "don't think I didn't! Just because you two are bloody dating doesn't mean you know everything. Not! At! All! And have you ever stopped to think that maybe all your cuddling and smooching and canoodling makes the rest of us feel just a little bit awkward and uncomfortable? We all used to be mates long before you two started going out, you know. And maybe we liked how it was before. You ever stop to think about that, eh?" Pearl's jaw finally shuts with a self-satisfied snap.

For a brief moment I feel disorientated and confused, like I've been sucked into some bizarre space warp. The four faces around me certainly look familiar, but my little secure world is suddenly changed and for a short while I can't seem to work out what or who fits where. Do our friends really feel this way? Don't they realize that this could ruin everything?

"What's that about then?" Toby calmly asks, flicking his gaze between Fran and Tom-Tom. He doesn't seem interested in hearing any more of Pearl's thoughts on the subject.

"Oh, Pearl . . ." Tom-Tom grimaces and shakes his head at the ground.

"Don't you '*Oh, Pearl*' me! You know it's true."

"Is it?" I finally speak, looking directly at Fran. She's my closest girlfriend; I trust her with the truth.

Fran gives a deep sigh, tilts her eyes up to the heavens and sends them plummeting back down to Earth frozen with an icy glare meant for Pearl. "Well . . . I suppose now that you two are a couple things have changed just a little," she says evenly. "They're bound to, aren't they? But change isn't necessarily a bad thing, now is it?" Her voice has a soothing, final quality to it, like she's hoping this simple explanation will diffuse the bomb and we can all potter on as before.

The sound of children laughing and bawdy skaters terrorizing the English language laps at the silence. Right now I think Fran would appreciate a reassuring comment from Tom-Tom to seal the deal, but she might as well wish for a hunk-of-the-month sandwich because Tom is doing the typical blokey thing and inspecting his fingernails like they hold the key to life's meaning.

"Yes, change can be a very good thing," Toby says steadily, "just like supportive mates." Pearl purses her lips haughtily and for once has the sense not to open her mouth.

"Exactly!" pips Tom-Tom, which makes

Frannie scowl. The air around us is charged with friction and crackling like a sub-station.

"You Tom then?" demands a brand-new voice on the scene. The sound is rumbling and heavy and smashes the tension between us like a marble landing on glass. The sudden appearance of an intruder has destroyed the angry moment and instantly united us. Our heads snap back in synchronised unison and we squint up at the strange deep voice.

"Who are you?" is Tom-Tom's reply.

"A question for a question. *So* twenty-first century man! Suspicion—a sign of the times, I guess. Name's Lucas. Just wanted to say I dig your website. Verrrrry cool."

The sky above is stained with moldy layers of stratus clouds that have been hanging about for days, and they highlight the long rusty hair of the deep voice called Lucas like a halo. His sentences are short, like statements or small bursts of energy.

"You do? That's good to hear." Tom-Tom sounds chuffed.

"There were a few postings from some loonies, mind you," Lucas continues. "How about that April Tucker person? Some folks have more gaga imagination than brain cells. Ho ho. And I thought I was weird!"

You are *weird*, I think to myself sulkily. And so what, it was for a good cause. We *all* decided to post something to get the website started, it's not like I was looking for attention. But I don't actually say anything and just glare up at the red circle of light that is Lucas's head with the meanest expression I can find instead.

"Yup, you sure get 'em," Lucas concludes, crossing his arms and rolling gently on his toes and heels with his shoulders all bunched up. He doesn't seem to be leaving.

"Um, you want to sit down for a minute?" Tom-Tom offers.

"Mmm. Okay then." He yawns. His attitude seems a little too nonchalant to be genuine and I get the impression that his casual, couldn't-care-less manner is staged. He certainly seems cool and cocksure, but his confidence comes across as a well-rehearsed act and seems defensive rather than something that is natural to him. Toby says I stare, but this is just me taking careful note of people.

Lucas sits down with his daddy long legs crossed and we all shift about to make room for him. Not that it helps much, his hard sharp knees are still around his ears. I can see him a lot better without the dazzling backdrop of clouds and the first thing I notice is his smile. It's broken. It doesn't reach his eyes and it's straight instead of curved and hard where it should be soft and creased. I wonder if he knows it's broken.

"I think I've seen you around . . . you go to Dunton Secondary, huh?" Tom-Tom revs the silence.

"I did. I left just before my A Levels. I thought, what's the point?"

"That's *exactly* what *I* say!" Pearl caws with her face all lit up like a lighthouse. She's elated that finally somebody else in the world makes sense too. But Pearl's opinion on anything is just about the last thing I need right now, so I quickly steer the conversation away from her and her silly insights.

"So what do you do now?" I quickly ask Lucas.

"I play guitar. Putting a band together . . ."

"Cool," I say and bob my head. "What sort of band are you then?"

"So far we're just a guitar. Ha ha. I'm still auditioning other musicians. I'm really into the whole folk-rock thing though."

"Cool," we all murmur. The sound of children and skaters suddenly seems very loud again.

"Oh, I remember you now!" Pearl suddenly exclaims. "You were two years ahead of us. I used to see you sitting all alone playing your guitar on the field during breaks." Pearl couldn't even spell tact.

"Yeah," Lucas drawls indifferently, "I wasn't into hanging out with those cretins in my year. And music is my life."

"That's what Archie says," Pearl continues, tightening her lips, "except he's in a marching band."

Poor Archie, I groan inwardly. I feel a certain connection with him since our triple date on Friday.

"I know you like Archie!" Pearl roars. She obviously caught my groan. "But then of course *you* would. He was—after all—the only one who didn't laugh hysterically at your getup for the cinema."

Suddenly the whole group looks perky again; even Toby's mouth is twitching. I have a horrible sense of foreboding and I'm just about to explain —for the zillionth time—that I did it for Anna, but Pearl is quicker on the draw.

"Ha ha, you'll enjoy this one, Lucas. Ella got herself all dolled up for our triple date to the movies on Friday—hair wild, boots, glittery lips, false nails—picture it . . . the whole shebang!

Anyway, I don't know WHAT she and Toby were doing beforehand, but by the time they met us at the movies Toby was walking around with one of her falsies dangling in his hair. And he didn't even know it!"

"Yes, thanks for that. . . ." I attempt, but Pearl cuts me off.

"But *Ella knew*, and she was standing behind Toby silently pleading with us all to keep quiet." While she's describing the event Pearl mimics me putting my finger to my lips and frantically eyeball-begging. I obviously wasn't thinking at the time; Pearl couldn't keep a secret if her collection of Wonderbras depended on it.

Sitting there listening to her recount the whole sorry episode is like reliving it again and again, and the memory of Toby and me walking the rest of the way to the movies—with me casually trying to swat the fingernail from his hair—plays over and over in my mind like a rerun of a bad comedy. But Toby wasn't buying my flies-in-winter story, nor was he interested in my demonstration on how he should get his hair cut. I certainly learned something about Toby that night: he doesn't like having his head touched. So much for the fingers-through-the-hair experience then.

By the time Pearl concludes her narration the entire group, including new-boy Lucas, is chuckling manically. I certainly wouldn't laugh at somebody I had just met, that's just rude (and a worthy Good Sense Guide quote if I ever heard one)! My face is as hot and red as a fever and I feel dead silly all over again. Not really because of the falsie-in-the-hair thing, but rather because it's so blatantly obvious that I was trying to impress Toby. And that's just seriously sad.

"I already told you, Anna . . . Marks & Sparks . . . big sister routine . . . blah blah," but everybody is giggling too much to notice my stammering and I might as well be explaining myself to a brick. If Anna was here right now I'd definitely give her that finger-flick between the eyes!

"So where do you live, Luc-Arse?" I ask, holding a sickly-sweet smile up to my face. Not that I care, but I'm desperate to change the subject. And I hope he's noticed that I've changed his name to rhyme with arse, because that's what I think he is for laughing at me.

"Just up the road," he replies, drying his crying eyes.

A *donkey's arse*, to put a point on it.

Chapter 9
Litter Space Bug

Toby and I have finally received a response to our dog-walking flyers. Miss Tilburn, who owns Dunton's secondhand bookshop called Bookends and lives in the flat above, is going to be our very first customer. I've never actually been inside the shop but I can't recall a day when it wasn't around. I've never met Miss Tilburn either, but Mum is a Bookends regular and describes her as a bit of a recluse. I'm hoping she's an eccentric too; I've never met a proper one before. Toby and I have arranged to stop by her shop on our way home from school today so that we can meet her (and the dog), and discuss some sort of walking schedule. It's all very businesslike and I think I may get the hang of this part-time job thing.

As we step inside the shop's gloomy cavity, a dangling copper windchime above the door tinkles our arrival. The room is small and claustrophobic and the walls climb all over me, making me wish I was outside again. It doesn't take very long to absorb the floor-to-ceiling bookshelves burdened with jumbles of books that don't seem to be jammed in any particular order. There's very little else to the shop, although there is a stained-glass reading lamp that shares an antique desk with an old, engraved metal cash register in the corner. The rest of the space is dim and colorless and powered by watery light that has managed to sift in through the shop's dirty front window.

"It smells like something died in here," Toby whispers through a crack in his lips.

"Shh. She'll hear you," I hiss, spying a woman with dark hair and a long pale skirt perched on a tall, sturdy-looking A-frame stepladder. She's not alone; there's a frail old man standing at the foot of the ladder holding it stable for her. *He doesn't look very strong but he's obviously a gentleman*, I think to myself before I realize that he's actually staring right up her big billowy umbrella skirt. I give Toby wide *Twilight Zone* eyes and notice that his are as huge as my own. He's also spotted Mr. Peeping Tom!

"Right . . ." says the woman, as she begins her descent down the ladder. They haven't noticed Toby and me standing there. Somebody needs to upgrade the windchime to something electronic, it seems. The old man coughs and shuffles back a few paces to give the woman and her skirt space to land. "There you go, Henry," she smiles patiently and hands him the book, which is brown, just like everything else in the shop. "Now that's the very last one I have on D-Day. If you're not happy with this one then I'm afraid I can't help you. It doesn't have a dust jacket, mind you, but at one pound fifty we can't complain, now can we?"

The old man shakes his head agreeably and swaps the book for some coins from his pocket without saying a word. As he turns around to leave he almost collides with Toby and me, which is when I notice that he's wearing thick bottle-top glasses that magnify his eyes right out of proportion, like a creature with giant, compound eyes.

"Oh, do excuse me, Colonel," he says and tips his head apologetically. I was winding up for a filthy I-know-what-you-were-up-to glare, but now realizing that he couldn't actually see a thing I offer a friendly smile as compensation.

"Yes?" The woman finally turns to acknowledge us. Her hair is thick and dark and neatly bobbed and although her skin is quite smooth, the deep furrows running between her nostrils and the corners of her mouth point to her being on the downhill slope of middle age. She's wearing a soft lavender-colored blouse with puffed-up sleeves and a large scalloped collar that's held in place by two strategic dragonfly buttons. I'm quite sure she made the blouse herself; I've never seen another one quite like it.

"I'm Ella Watson," I blurt out, "and this is Toby Sinclair."

"And I'm Maggie Tilburn. How is your mum?" she asks.

"Er, she's fine. You called us about walking your dog?"

"That's correct," she replies, like this is a game of true or false. As she stands there staring at us expectantly I notice that she has the palest blue eyes I've ever seen. They're so pale they make my own eyes hurt.

"Yes, um . . . well, so how would you like your dog walked? I mean, how often?" So I've never done this before.

"Ah, perhaps you should meet Laika first," she says and turns in the direction of the desk. "Laika was the first dog in space, you know."

I give Toby a skewed look; my first eccentric! "Riiiggght..." we chime in unison, and follow her.

Miss Tilburn disappears behind the desk for a few moments and once again emerges holding something small, brown and fluffy. "Not my Laika, mind you. That Laika was a Russian stray dog that was launched into orbit in 1957 aboard the *Sputnik II*. My little Laika," she says, stroking the brown fluff and chuckling daintily to herself, "hasn't even been out of Dunton. Have you, baby girl? Nooooo you haven't! No no no no no."

I think she's forgotten we're here. The dog, I also notice, is a Pekinese. It has big ears and bulbous bug-eyes and looks just like a gremlin. Toby is giving it the once-over too, and doesn't seem particularly impressed. I think he imagined himself striding through town with the impressive fangs of a German shepherd at the end of a lead. I don't think he envisaged taking Gizmo for a walk out in public.

"Laika darling, these lovely young people are going to take you for a walkies. What do you think about that?" Laika stares at us without blinking for a few moments, and then slowly draws her lip up—like the ceremonious raising of a stage curtain—until her entire top row of teeth is bared and her black nose is bunched up like a wrinkled prune. Finally a low growl rumbles from her belly. Laika, it seems, is not taken with the idea. "She'll warm to you," says Miss Tilburn, nonplussed. "She must! She has a bad ticker and needs to lose a bit of weight, for her own good."

"And *you* haven't thought about walking her?" Toby asks, looking decidedly uneasy about the whole situation. I respond with a withering look that says it all: great business strategy, Toby.

"Come on, let's see you go for a trial walk—a quick around-the-block," suggests Miss Tilburn, placing Laika on the floor and ignoring Toby's suggestion entirely. "Go on, take it," she squeaks, jiggling the end of the dog lead in our general direction. Her pale eyes have gone all shiny and her face has the strained look of someone who's giving up their only child for adoption.

Right now I feel like I'm the only person in this room who still has a firm grasp on their senses and reality, so I take the lead and attempt to focus on the snarling ball of fluff with stick-out eyes greedily contemplating my feet like they're the main course. "Come along then . . . er." I can't remember the space-dog's name.

"Laika," Toby chirps. He's got his hands in his pockets and is suddenly very smug.

"Yeah, thanks for that," I reply, giving him a

look very similar to the one Laika is giving me.

"Come on, girl." *Like her, Like her*, I say over and over in my head. I start walking in the direction of the door and Laika miraculously follows.

"See you in a few minutes," I hear Miss Tilburn calling after us nervously as we step out onto the High Street pavement. "Toodle-oo, then . . ."

"Are you useless or what?" I grumble at Toby once we're out of earshot.

"You handle the small ones and I'll be in charge of the bigger hounds," he grins, looking self-satisfied and stress-free as he strides on ahead. Laika amazingly continues walking for a few steps but then suddenly decides to stop and sit. Even though I never told her to. This dog needs training.

"Or," I shout after Toby, "we could just go around encouraging people to walk their own dogs. Now that's bound to make us a fortune." Of course I'm still a lady in love, only right now I'm a seriously annoyed one. Everything about the last fifteen minutes is just plain weird.

"Around the block, remember? Now come along," Toby sings happily. He's not really that happy, he's just trying to annoy me.

"Come on, little bug-eyes," I say encouragingly, "get your fluffy rump moving." That's the upside of talking to dogs; as long as your tone is soothing you really can say whatever you want. "You know, if they can put one man on the moon," I continue, loud enough for Toby to hear, "I really don't see why they don't put the whole lot of them up there." I give the lead a gentle tug and Laika finally stands up, but she's simply toying with me and won't shift another inch. "Oh, please come on!" I plead, crouching down to her level. And that's when I notice it. Her furry face is wrinkled with concentration and her bulgy eyes are half-mast and somewhere distant. And then I smell it . . . dog doo!

"You're not . . . ?" I cry out. But she is. And she looks very happy with herself for doing so too. *Now* she'll walk.

"You're not leaving that there, are you missy?"

I spin around to find a policeman all crisp and polished in his black uniform.

"It's not my dog!"

"He's on your lead."

"It's not even my lead. I'm the dog-walker . . . the trial dog-walker, that is." I fade out, realizing how idiotic I sound.

"If you're the dog-walker then you're responsible for the poopy," the policeman announces loudly, like he's hoping we can *all*—the nosy high street shoppers included—take something positive away from this experience.

Poopy? What am I, like five years old? And can I pass you a loud hailer, because I think a few hard-of-hearing pensioners at Shady Pines missed your community broadcast about dog *poopy*.

"I don't have a poop . . . bag," I mutter dismally. I almost said "poopy." I stare around at the shaking heads of the high street shoppers, hoping to see only strangers. Fat freaking chance! My snooty sister Anna is standing there, looking as bright and shiny as a red apple, although her poncy best mate Marcia seems to be enjoying herself. When I'm free I'm moving to a very large city.

"I'm sure one of these shops won't mind donating a plastic bag or two," the policeman rattles on, gesturing authoritatively at the shop fronts lining the street.

Finally Toby steps in. "I'll get a bag, don't worry—we'll sort this out," he says. I stare at him with a face that's calm and expressionless. I hope he doesn't think he's suddenly jumping on board to save the day, because he missed that boat by about ten minutes.

"Well, then . . . mind you do," the policeman finally utters, and turns away reluctantly. I think he was hoping to call for backup.

I don't dare root out Anna again and stand there with one hand on my hip and the other clutching the wretched dog lead, staring up at nothing in particular while I wait for Toby and the you-know-what bag to appear. Why do stupid things always happen to me? I'll tell me why, it's because I'm always doing stupid things for other people. Like wearing falsies to make Anna happy, and walking the furry space bug because Toby—my so-called *boyf*—is too cool to be seen with it. Pah! We've all got to stand by our decisions, but you only have to make a mistake once to learn the lesson. This is the last time I look the fool. There's loads of good sense in that.

Chapter 10
Love Bytes

I've decided to forgive Toby. He's just too buff and funny and lovely not to. Plus I love him. And I suppose he did come to the rescue with a few plastic bags from Togs for Tots, although I still gave him the silent treatment all the way home. I'd like to think I stood my ground. And if I've learned anything it's that the best thing about an argument (even if it's the worst type: a silent one), is making up again afterward. We kissed for about ten minutes.

It's second break and I'm caught between getting stuck into a girly chat with Frannie and Pearl, and watching Toby play soccer. Not that I'm really into the sport, but I could sit and watch Toby forever. I'd rather he was cuddling up with me, of course, but I suppose he needs his blokey time. And I don't want to be the clingy sort; I've got to retain some mystery about me.

"I'm so glad you share my joy, Ella Mental!"

"Pardon," I mumble, dragging my eyeballs kicking and screaming from the soccer game. I think Pearl just said something. Or maybe it was Frannie.

"I don't know why you even bother hanging out with us. It's quite obvious you find Toby Sinclair a lot more interesting." That was Pearl. Here we go again.

"Not at all," I say brightly. "And I was watching Tom-Tom actually—he's having a really good game." I've worked out the Good Sense Guide to telling lies, remember?

"You wouldn't know a good game of soccer if it hit you between the eyes." She sighs petulantly. That's true, I can't argue with that.

"Pearl's met some hot totty on the Internet." Fran steps in between the looming squabble. "He's eighteen years old, he's called Simon, and they met on an Internet chat site called TeenChat." She's memorized all the key words. Good move.

"I can speak for myself, you know." Pearl sulks, but then quickly forgets to. "Yes, the site is called TeenChat, his name is Simon and he's studying at St Andrew's University, which is in Scotland. He's a language whiz and loves polo, poetry, and sailing. We've talked about everything under the sun and it's like we were made for each other. And he's gorgeous!"

"So you've met, have you?" I ask with genuine interest.

Pearl responds with a look I can only describe as foul and withering. Ah, we seem to have discussed this already then.

"No she hasn't, but he's six foot one with black hair and blue eyes and rides a motorbike," Frannie slides in for her second save of the day. How she manages to keep a straight face as she says this I just don't know, although the smile tripping around the corners of her eyes is hard to miss. This Simon sounds a bit like Rick in *Wings of Desire*, and I'm almost willing to bet that he's just that: entirely fictional. But I don't dare say that to Pearl or she'll have my liver for lunch. Frannie's also skeptical, but she's too much of a coward to say anything. As it turns out, so am I.

"Cool!" I gush pathetically. "So how long have you two been e-mailing each other?"

"We only 'met' a few weeks ago, but it's been more intense and special than any relationship I've ever had before. And he says I'm the most incredible person he's ever met. We just clicked from the moment we logged on and found each other. It was fate!"

Fate? Oh, gag! But I try my best to look interested and bob my head with every word.

"He hasn't been able to e-mail me a photo yet, but he says that his last girlfriend—they went out for three years, so he's definitely not into short relationships—described him as 'surfer sexy meets Wall Street style.'" Pearl sighs, clearly smitten. "I sent him two photos of me. I was originally going to send him the photo of me in my red dress, but he said he wanted one of me in my school uniform instead. He said he wants to picture me as I really am, every day. He's sooo romantic! So I sent him both. Anyway, if all goes according to plan we should hopefully meet up in a few weeks' time."

I can't imagine why a brainy, drop-dead eighteen-year-old would need to meet girls over the Internet. Surfer sexy meets Wall Street style? I bet he's more bulldog meets Pekinese. But the shrill ring of the end-of-lunch bell saves me from having to paint over my skepticism, and as we trudge off to our next class I sneak Fran an exaggerated sigh. Something tells me the next Pearlodrama has just been scheduled.

Mum and Anna have been arguing over the phone bill for the last few days, but they've obviously made up because when I arrive home from school I find them sharing a sandwich and Mum hiccuping with laughter.

"What are you doing home early then?" I ask Mum. It's like Dad says, you have to work to put food on the table—it doesn't fly there on its own.

"Anna has a photo shoot later today, so I've taken the afternoon off," she replies, still grinning. Whatever they were laughing about must have been hysterical.

"Whatever . . . " I murmur at no one in particular and start the hike upstairs to the blissful solitude that is my bedroom. No Anna-lovers there!

"I heard about Miss Tilburn's Pekinese," Mum calls after me. I stop mid-step and contemplate whether she's referring to the fact that I took the furry space bug for a trial walk, or that I was practically arrested for its pavement *poopy*. I don't know why I even bother wasting my time with optimism; she can barely get her words past the giggles, which makes the answer fairly obvious I think. I remain still and silent for a few seconds—burning to say something brilliant and intelligent that will shut them both up once and for all, but my brain is a spaghetti junction of noisy, uncontrollable thoughts. I'm just too irritated to think clearly.

"At least I have a boyfriend. . . ." I finally mumble, and continue the trudge upstairs to my bedroom. It's the best I could come up with. I need some time alone to recharge. Spend some time alone every day, that's Good Sense Guide number thirty-six, if I'm not mistaken. I close my door and my schoolbag slips from my shoulder with a thump. Finally, my sanctuary from the world. This is my own special little hideaway and the only place where, for a while at least, I don't have to consider anybody or anything if I don't want to. I can just be. And just be me. This is where I come to find my peace and make my peace.

Knock. Knock.

Or it would be, if my sanctuary didn't share floor space with the rest of the Watson household. "Yes?" I sigh.

The door opens halfway. It's Mum's head. "Sorry I laughed at you, Ella."

Sure you are.

"But . . . well, you have to admit, it is a rather funny story."

What is the point in apologizing if you're going to carry it on? You're either sorry or you're not, but don't follow a *sorry* with a *but*! I don't, however, speak the words out loud and simply make a mental note to add it to my Good Sense Guide instead. Mum can read about it when it's published, just like everybody else.

"Anyway, I have some good news for you," she continues.

"Yeah, and what's that?"

"Dad says we can get the Internet at home."

"I'd say that's more family good news than Ella good news," I reply smugly. I don't mind being neglected, but don't expect me to do cartwheels for crumbs.

"Oh, Ella, we just can't please you, can we?"

I don't reply and simply sit there staring at my mum who seems to have it all figured out. I wonder what she'd say if she knew I'd found her worn-out naughty novels. I know why they call them bodice-rippers. I looked it up in the dictionary. And I know all her favorite bodice-ripping bits too—they're the pages the book always falls open on. The thought starts me giggling.

"What's so funny?" Mum asks.

"Nothing." I grin.

"You're a strange girl, Ella," she concludes as her shaking head disappears out the door.

In my world you're *the strange ones*, I brood

and move toward the framed picture of sunflowers hanging on the wall. I used to hide my diary with the Good Sense Guide underneath the tissues in my bedside tissue box, but I had a snoop called Anna so I had to be cunning and find a new hiding spot. I extract my treasured diary from behind the picture and flip to the last page with writing. I'm at Good Sense number thirty-seven already, which is just as well—because certain people are in desperate need of a guide to some seriously good sense!

I add the quote about saying sorry and quickly return my diary to the darkness. Since discovering Mum's "Hearts and Flowers" novels I've been neglecting *CosmoGIRL!*, in fact I'm two issues behind already. Still, I have the latest one on hand and an entire afternoon without Anna and her fan club to disturb me.

Chapter 11
Class Act

Our school's amateur dramatics society is putting on a stage production of *Grease* at the local theatre in aid of the Unicorn Children's Foundation, and we're all going along to support the worthwhile cause. I'm really looking forward to it. Not only is there the feel-good factor that goes along with supporting a charity, but I've also seen the movie *Grease*—the one with John Travolta—like a thousand times and I know all the words to all the songs.

Thanks to Miss Tilburn and her space bug, Toby and I are now sitting in Gary's Grill and enjoying a romantic burger before we meet up with the rest of our mates at the local theatre. At least we got paid for my humiliation.

"I love all the songs," I continue, "but 'Hopelessly Devoted to You' is definitely my favorite." I start humming it softly while I munch my chips, just to prove that not only do I know what I'm talking about, but I really *feel* the song too. I'm learning so much about romance from April and Misty.

"You know all the words?" Toby asks. He seems anxious.

"Uh huh, all of 'em," I say and take a straw-sip of my drink.

Toby exhales loudly just as his mobile beeps with a text message. He quickly presses the "read" button. It's from Tom-Tom.

IM WITH LUCAS. U
GUYS MIND IF I BRING
HIM ALONG 2NITE?

"I don't mind," Toby replies and looks at me expectantly.

I shrug disinterestedly and focus on my burger instead. I still haven't quite forgiven Luc-Arse for making fun of me, which—come to think of it—seems to be a favorite national pastime these days. Toby texts him a reply and then concentrates on making quick work of his burger. We sit in comfortable munching silence for a few moments before Toby speaks again.

"Do you get the feeling that everyone is having a bit of trouble adjusting to . . . things?"

"What things?" I ask.

"Well, *us*."

"Ah right. It's not a feeling, they've come right out and admitted it, haven't they."

"Yeah, I guess so," he replies, and looks bothered.

I return my half-eaten burger to my plate and focus on wiping my fingers on a Gary's Grill paper napkin. This is probably a subject that needs some discussing.

"So how should we handle this?" I ask carefully.

"I'm really not sure." We spend the next few moments silently considering the situation with matching knotty foreheads.

"Well, maybe they need a little more time to adjust. We should probably just be patient and in the meantime try and make it less of a big deal," I reluctantly suggest. The thought leaves me feeling slightly frustrated—love is not something that should have a lid on it, but I love my mates too. When did this all get so complicated?

"You mean like ease up on the whole girlfriend-boyfriend thing while they're around?" Toby asks.

"Uh, I guess so." No need to take this to extremes though.

"I think I see what you mean. We need to show them that just because things between you and me have changed, it won't necessarily affect our relationship as a group."

"Exactly." I nod, trying to shoo away the tiny sliver of resentment stealthily creeping its way into my head. It's not often you get Toby talking about feelings and relationships, and I had rather hoped that when he did start talking it wouldn't be about cooling things down. But I do see his point, and I don't want Toby at the expense of my other mates. It's easy to take mates for granted and just assume that they'll always be around. I don't want to make that mistake; that's definitely Good Sense Guide logic. Sometimes the depth of my wisdom is quite startling. I think it may even be bottomless.

Fran and Pearl are loitering patiently outside the theatre and serve as guiding beacons for Toby and me who cruise in from the left, and Tom-Tom and Lucas, who glide in from the right. We come together in a circle formation and quickly settle into our hellos and general chit-chat like we were never even apart. Toby and I make a conscious point of not touching and I take care not to catch his eye or send him private looks. I used to send him private looks when he was just a boy and my friend (and not my *boyfriend*) mind you, but I suppose everyone thinks that these looks carry special significance now. Which they would do, if everybody would just stop getting in the way.

I decide to redirect my thoughts to Lucas, before they get all twisted up. He's just as bold as he ever was, but somehow his confidence doesn't seem quite so edgy any more. Tonight he seems a little softer, like he's still convinced that he's one helluva guy, only this time he's hoping we'll all see it too. He's a teensier bit more attentive and appears to be making an effort to go with the flow of conversation, rather than riding haughtily on its crest. I think he wants very desperately to be our friend. And I guess that makes me want to like him.

He's taller than I remember; a good head above Toby. And what a head of dark rusty curls that is, I notice. He's also very bony. His clothes hang from his body like a shapeless shroud, loosely billowing with empty folds that should be filled out with soft, fleshy bulges.

"The show starts in twenty minutes—shall we head inside?" Tom-Tom asks, sizing up the shrinking queue. We all nod and begin trailing in the direction of the ticket booth.

The theatre foyer is small and smells musty,

which may have something to do with the old brown and burgundy carpet crunching underfoot. The area to our left is taken up almost entirely by a snack bar selling crisps, cold drinks, and sweets as well as a few neglected hotdogs, nachos, and sausage rolls that are nestling inside a glass warming-oven, still waiting patiently to be picked. The end of the counter is devoted to a drinks bar complete with beer mats and plastic ashtrays with logos. The chalkboard offers wine from cartons, an assortment of spirit miniatures, and beer bottles to anybody who can prove they're over eighteen.

I may be burgered out but I still have a small space left for chocolate. There's always space for chocolate, it has its own reserved sign. I instinctively turn to ask Toby if he wants something, but then remember that we're not supposed to be doing the girlfriend-boyfriend thing. This is stupid, even in our pre-loved-up days I'd have asked Toby if he fancied a snack (that's what you do for best mates), but now I'm being forced to go to abnormal extremes. We're supposed to be acting like nothing is different, but it seems as if everything is different . . . which it's not supposed to be. I'm really confused.

"What have you got there?" Pearl asks.

"Chocolate," I sulk and open the packet immediately. I need some comforting. "What are you going to have?"

"Nothing," replies Pearl. "I'm on a diet."

Ah, no doubt this has something to do with surfer-sexy-meets-Wall-Street Simon, I think to myself and shove a dark chocolatey drop in my mouth.

"Well, give us one," says Pearl, dipping her hand into the bag.

"I thought you were on a diet?"

"I am," she replies and pops the sweetness into her mouth.

"So nicking *other* people's calories doesn't count then?"

But Pearl's not listening and she sashays over to Lucas who is cradling a cardboard tray of steaming nachos. Toby has also sniffed out the nachos and is offering to swap one for a toffee.

Yoo hoo . . . I have chocolate. I rattle the bag of chocs like I'm collecting small change, but Toby doesn't seem to notice. I don't remember him not noticing me before. What happens if we extinguish the fire of our love by neglecting it? I suddenly panic. That's what almost happened to Tucker and April in *Flames of Passion*. Could it be that we're being a little too severe with our decision to cool things down in front of our mates? You can't go from all to nothing in one day, it's not natural. A bit of eyeball lovey-dovey would be okay, surely? *CosmoGIRL!* says that if you catch your man's eye three times you're sending out a message. And if you catch his eye and hold the look and smile, well, that's like the ultimate eyeball flirt. And if I can't tempt him with my chocolate, then I have no choice but to resort to drastic measures.

Unfortunately I'm not a person who is effortlessly good at anything. I have to work at most things. I get good grades, but I study for them. I have okay skin, but I have to cleanse, tone and moisturize to a schedule. And as for this acting sexy business, well that's not coming naturally to me either. I lower my chin coyly, plump up my lips and sneak a peak at Toby through fluttering eyelashes. He's still got his nose in Lucas's nachos, but I continue staring—visualising my pupils as red-hot lasers. For a while nothing happens, but just as I'm beginning to feel extremely silly Toby suddenly spins around and collides with my gaze. He looks confused.

I can feel a crimson glow seeping out across my cheeks and down my neck, but I don't look away and keep focused on my instructions from *CosmoGIRL!*. I continue staring, and then slowly roll my lips out into a seductive smile. I'm not entirely sure what a seductive smile is, to be honest—but I try to do the Hollywood thing and make sure every one of my teeth are showing. Toby doesn't budge and after a while his confusion morphs into impatience. He's looking at me like I'm on day release from the loony bin. Finally he comes over to me.

"Are you okay?"

"What do you mean?" I grin triumphantly.

"You look like you're in pain." He's starting to sound irritated.

"No. But, er . . . I do have chocolate," I offer hopefully.

"Come on, babes—we agreed we'd chill with our mates. We'll hang out together tomorrow, okay?"

Toby's never called me "babes" before—it's definitely something, and so I nod enthusiastically. I have a nasty suspicion I'm acting like a complete idiot. Love seems to have usurped my brain and put my heart in charge, which is quite obviously not a good idea. In fact, it's a very bad swap. I'll have to keep a closer eye on love next time.

Chapter 12
Fire and Rain

I think my good sense has finally returned to me; I didn't sing a single word to any of the songs during the performance of *Grease*. Not even to "Hopelessly Devoted to You" (*especially* not to "Hopelessly Devoted to You"!). I was very cool and Toby seemed less frightened. I think I'm getting the hang of this. Right now, I'm at the local library using their Internet facilities. Dad says we should be connected by the weekend, but then he also said we'd get two extra movie channels for the winter, so I won't count on it until I can see it with my own two eyeballs.

It's been a few weeks since I last visited Tom-Tom's PPT website, and the number of visitors has skyrocketed. Most of the postings are from kids who have also been bullied, and each one is very passionate and outspoken. When your days and weeks are spent sidestepping and kowtowing to those who are big, bad, or bitter you need an opportunity to vent anonymously and feel brave, I suppose.

There's a posting from somebody called Cyberpunk, who admits to being a reformed bully but says that the only reason he bullied was to avoid being the victim of bullying himself. "You either bully or you're bullied," he believes, which of course ignites everyone else with outrage and wild fury. Most call him a "saddo" and tell him to "grow a backbone," others say that he's "beneath contempt" and "no better than the rest of them." Cyberpunk hasn't replied.

As I scroll through the messages—reading as I go along—all I can think about is how lost we all are. Nobody has any of the answers really. We're all just fighting for survival and trying to figure it out as we go along. But why do we insist on making it so much harder for each other? Perhaps it is the strongest who survive, which might be what Cyberpunk was getting at. But wouldn't it be nice if they used their strength to protect rather than hurt those less brave or bold than themselves? Isn't that why they're the strong ones in the first place?

Leaving Cyberpunk and his challengers behind I unintentionally stumble across a posting from someone called Tin Man. I read his words over and over again until my throat is tight and my eyes are clammy; his sadness is as gray and heavy as a lead sinker.

> H'lo Peeps,
> I wake up in the morning soaked in numbness. I feel nothing. No sadness or happiness. I just am. So what do you do with yourself when you have nothing inside you? When your humanness has left you? I try to cover it up, but everybody sees that I'm empty. Still, they can laugh and ridicule all they want. Remember, I feel nothing.
> S'long,
> Tin Man

There are no replies to this posting and I can't say that I'm surprised; that's anguish on a level thankfully very few of us can relate to. Still, it seems wrong to leave him alone with his emptiness. As I sit there contemplating a reply suddenly someone—or something—grabs my shoulders. I hear a shriek (I think it might be my own) and levitate in the air for what feels like minutes. By the time I finally hit my chair again I have a faint pulse but my heart is still cowering and pressed up tightly against my ribcage for support. Who . . . what . . . why . . . ?

I'm still in the public library, which is good news, although everyone is gawping at me—not such good news. But reassured by their presence I turn around to face the shoulder-grabber. It's Lucas, and he's grinning at me awkwardly. All of a sudden the head librarian appears behind him. She's fizzing with anger.

"This is a library," she snaps, "not a playground. Out! The pair of you! This very minute!" This starts the gawpers sniggering quietly out of their nostrils like they've sprung leaks.

"But I didn't even do anything wrong," I whisper hoarsely, making a last-ditch attempt to prove to her that I do actually know my library rules.

"I said out!" she repeats and jabs her head-librarian finger in the direction of the automatic doors. I want to screech out in protest but I don't have the nerve to and I snatch up my schoolbag and flounce in the direction of her finger instead. I make it outside and discover Lucas standing right beside me.

"Er, sorry, Ella," he says, smiling his broken smile. "I didn't think you'd scream."

"I so don't think I screamed. But what were you expecting?" I'm aiming for a furious growl but it comes out sounding more like an exasperated sigh instead. He looks so embarrassed, and I don't want to add to that, although I am still irritated by this strange new boy who seems to turn up everywhere unannounced. "So what were you doing in the library then?" I ask. Stupid question, but I'm making a stab at normal conversation.

"Looking for books?"

"I figured as much," I reply evenly (deep breath), "but what sort of books?"

"Books on music . . . sheet music, mostly," he adds eagerly. This time his tone is thick and warm, as if he's trying to smooth over the damage and stop me from turning away.

"Oh, that's cool." I nod with rock-chick aplomb, like sheet music is something I can dig. Lucas gives me a concurring nod, like we're kindred spirits bound by our love of the beat. Silence. Now we're both staring at one another.

I'm not entirely sure what has just taken place here, but I feel as though we've been doing an elaborate social dance around each other, gently prodding at our respective boundaries to gauge the shape of our characters. And with that out the way, we now seem comfortable enough to move on to the next phase of this getting-to-know-you ritual.

"So where are you off to then?" Lucas asks.

"I have to head home. I have control-freak parental units who do homework inspections and odd things like that," I explain, feeling bad that I'm so boring.

"Ah, right," he responds. "I thought I might go and visit Tom."

"I sort of live in that direction, we could walk together for a bit if you like?"

Lucas nods and we set off side by side, him walking in slow giant strides with his rusty curls trailing behind him and me chugging along beside him with my legs working overtime.

"Do you live with your folks?" I ask, eager to hotwire this conversation and leave the silence behind us.

"Yup, although not for much longer if they have their way," he replies. "They were less than pleased when I left school. And they're even more fed up with the fact that I'm not studying or working now either."

I reckon his units probably have a point, but I don't know Lucas well enough to say so. "What are you planning on doing then?" I ask instead.

"I'm going to be a musician. I'm teaching myself to play the guitar and as for the rest of it, I reckon you either have the talent or you don't. You can't go to school to learn a gift. And as for a job, I've already applied with the Council to train as a tree surgeon but I take medication so that sort of gets in the way of things—high-powered machinery especially. Ha ha ha."

"Ha ha . . . er." Sigh. Now what? Of course part of me wants to know more, but what about respecting people's privacy and blissful ignorance and too much awkward freaking information? But then what else is relevant to this conversation? Think!

"What sort of medication?" I finally mumble.

"I have bipolar disorder," he offers casually. "It's nothing major and I'm learning to control it, with medication. I guess I'm just a moody bastard," he concludes with a wry chuckle and then looks to me for confirmation . . . or some sort of reaction, I'm really not sure."

"Ah, right," I say. I've never met anybody with bipolar disorder and I don't actually know what it is. I suppose I could ask, but it doesn't seem right to expect a sick person to give vivid details of an illness they would probably rather forget about. I'll have to look bipolar disorder up on the Internet later, but for now I must walk a careful line between so-what and gross fascination. "So how long have you had the disorder for?" That seems like a safe question.

"It's difficult to say really. It's not like one day you're fine and dandy and then the next day you're bipolar. It's just something that develops over time. The doctors say it's a chemical thing—in your brain."

"Ah right."

"Personally I think it's down to the fact that I was born in a storm," he continues, not in the least bit shy or put off by my ignorance, "one of the worst storms in British history, to be exact. Almost seventeen years ago, winds and rain lashed the entire country. It was dark for nearly two days. Floods were reported almost everywhere. Cars and trucks were blown over. Animals that didn't drown died of fright. Giant trees were snapped in half. And I came into the world. I had a crazy journey getting here—my wiring is bound to be a bit loose. What were they expecting? Ha ha ha."

I don't think I know what we're talking

about anymore, but I'm entranced by his boundless thoughts and high-voltage energy. I've never met anyone quite like Lucas before; he's like some tall, floaty spirit from another world and right now the most interesting thing to do is listen to everything he has to say. His mouth is smiling its broken smile and snickering softly, but as he turns to face me his dark eyes tell me that he'd do just about anything to be able to turn time right around again and come back into this world on a day that was calm and unremarkable. Being different can be tiring and lonely.

Chapter 13
Bird on a Wire

Toby and I made a pact to give our friends the time they need and I always keep my promises, especially those made to *mon amour* (which means "my love" in French—Misty spent a whole year in France). So I figured a girly afternoon was in order and Pearl suggested we hang out at her house. She wants to show us something, she says. This makes both me and Fran nervous, but I agreed on the grounds that:

1. Our local librarian has anger management issues.
2. Pearl has the Internet.
3. I'm still trying to learn about bipolar disorder.
4. Even though I'm a lady in love, I must spend time with my girlie mates.

I'm not entirely sure what Frannie's grounds are, but she was happy to go along with the plans. I know that she finds Pearl's family just as crazy as I do, which is not surprising considering that Fran is an only child and lives in a very ordered and sane household. Pearl has a really nice family, but they're a loud and lawless lot and stepping through their front door is a bit like walking into a hurricane. The only way to survive the experience is to keep your back against something solid, grabbing on tight when possible, and hold a keen eye out for flying objects—one flying object in particular: Pearl's younger brother Dirty Dan.

I don't know many ten-year-olds, but this one is as quick and wiry as a fox and obsessed with two things: peanut butter and wrestling (usually at the same time). His favorite trick is to lie in wait and pounce from a height and pin you to the floor in a takedown. I only know that it's called a takedown because that's what Dirty Dan shrieks when his peanut-butter breath lands on me. Nothing is funny when you're underneath it. And if the excruciating pain doesn't get you, the greasy peanut butter definitely will. Dan and his takedowns have ruined a skirt and two tops, one of which was Toby's favorite.

"I just know he's waiting for us," I whisper as Pearl fiddles with the front-door lock.

"You'd better tell him to back off, Pearl—he'll

listen to you," Fran adds nervously. I'm relieved I'm not alone with my fear.

"Don't worry, he wouldn't dare," Pearl scoffs. She may have a point; I don't know many people who would attempt a takedown on Pearl. Feeling slightly reassured, I follow her indoors but make sure I'm quick enough to get inside before Fran. I don't care how terrifying Pearl can be; I won't risk being the last one in.

"Don't even think about it, Dirty Dan!" Pearl yells out like she's communicating with ghosts. "I'll feed your testicles to the birds if you do."

The telly is on in the next-door living room and Fran and I remain huddled together, listening to the sound of a crowd roaring, somebody howling, and another voice counting to ten. Dan is definitely home. I glance up at the staircase and think I spy movement. I jab Fran with my elbow and signal with a jiggle of my eyebrows.

"Come on, you two," Pearl orders, impatient to get on with her show and tell. I gesture in the direction of the stairs and Pearl interprets my terror.

"Dan! You will appear! Now!"

Everything remains still and silent for a few seconds, and then Dan's brown, crusty grin slowly emerges from out of the shadows of the staircase landing. He has sticky-out, mad-scientist hair.

"Freak . . ." Pearl tut-tuts and then grabs us each by a sleeve to drag us upstairs and past the takedown *pea*-nut.

Pearl shares a bedroom with her younger sister, Beth, but we arrive to find the room Beth-*less*, which is probably just as well because Pearl always bulldozes the poor girl out into the hallway when we're there. We don't mind Beth one bit—she's cleaner and less dangerous than Dirty Dan, but Pearl likes to think of herself as the Queen of Cool, and hanging out with your little sis definitely does not fit the title.

"Okay, check this out." Pearl beams, pouncing on the wooden dining chair facing the table with the computer screen, which is open on the TeenChat homepage. She minimizes the website and opens up one of her Word folders, which she's entitled "Buff Bloke." Pearl does not do things in half measures and may just be descended from a block of cheese. Forget Queen of Cool, we're talking Princess of Parmesan, more like.

She's cut and pasted all the mails that have passed between her and surfer-sexy-meets-Wall-Street Simon over the past weeks and saved them in this special folder. She scrolls up to the top of the page and begins reading:

> (Buff Bloke says) hi there all u gorgiz gals out there im 18 yrs old 6 ft tall with black hair & blu eyes i drive a motorbike and im looking 2 meet stunning babes 4 fun friendship and maybe more any1 out there ;-)

"This is the first message he posted on TeenChat—the one I answered," Pearl explains.

"Buff Bloke—is that like his nickname?" I ask.

Pearl's face crumples with irritation. "No, it's not his nickname, dummo! His mates don't walk up to him in the street and shout 'Hi Buff Bloke!' do they? That's just his chat room name."

Whoa, have a coronary. You'd think I'd called him Barf Bag or something. "Oh," I say thoughtfully and bring my nose closer to the screen to focus on the next message.

> (Precious Pearl says) Hiya Buff Bloke. Could B I'm just what U R looking for. I'm 16 with long blonde hair & green eyes. I may B a schoolie but I reckon I

could teach U a thing or 2. So tell me more about yrself and we'll C if U make the grade!

"So you're Precious Pearl then?" Fran asks, quite obviously surprised by our friend's daring comeback.

"I reckon I could teach you a thing or two," I echo, reading from the screen. "What's that all about?"

"Oh don't be such a prude, Ella Mental Watson! It's only a bit of fun and anyway, now I have a gorgeous bloke who wants to go out with me. Well, he wants to meet me anyway."

"That's if he *is* gorgeous," I say. "Just because he says he's six foot and buff doesn't mean that he really is. Those are just words, Pearl. Anybody can write that. He might be a squat, pot-bellied pig with BO and halitosis for all you know."

Pearl glares at me with contempt and then demonstrates the V-sign with her two middle fingers. Unfortunately her message is not one of peace.

"Yeah, thanks for that—you can keep the change!" I snap back. Pearl can be a real charmer sometimes.

"Ella, if he's as disgusting as you seem to think he is then why would he want to meet me, huh? Yes, he wants to take me out. Read it and weep, girlfriend!" she sulks haughtily, scrolling down and jabbing a chipped crimson fingernail at the screen. The second-to-last entry is dated four days ago, almost two months after the first chat-room message.

> (Buff Bloke says) i cant take it anymore we have 2 meet u r definitely 1 of a kind i am coming to london soon and will let u know when i can come to dunton how abt getting 2gether

This Simon may be into polo, poetry, and sailing, but he's certainly not into punctuation and my eyeballs feel like they've come unhinged. Pearl responds to his message soon afterward.

> (Precious Pearl says) Sure can! Tell me when and where and I will B there! Can't wait! x

That's the final mail in the folder. Pearl continues salivating deliriously at the computer screen while Fran silently mouths the word *Pearlodrama* in my direction. She makes her eyes squint at the same time and I have to swallow hard to cork the laughter slinking up from my gullet. And Fran's right, we're definitely on a collision course with our next Pearlodrama. But so what if this Simon is pot-bellied! At least Pearl will learn her lesson about Internet chat rooms and being such a gullible chump. Pearl and reality really are very distant friends; maybe it's time the two become better acquainted. With all that said, there really is no point in Fran and me alienating ourselves from her when she's made up her mind, we're much better off staying on speaking terms with our troublesome friend. And I suppose it has been a while since our last Pearlodrama.

"That's cool, Pearl. Uh . . . I mean, Precious Pearl." I laugh with my face cracked open like a boiled egg.

"So how are things going with Toby then?" Fran asks, skipping from the subject of Pearl's love life to my own.

"Fine," I respond casually and begin a routine examination of my thumbnail. Of course I would do anything to have a good old girly natter about my *raison d'être* (which is French for my "reason for being"—another credit to Misty and obviously a reference to my Toby), but a deal's a deal. We said we were going to act as if nothing has changed, and that's what I'll do. Even if it kills me. Which it just might. I feel like I've won the lottery but can't tell anyone. I mean, what's the point of having a boyfriend if you can't talk about him all the time! This is all very cruel and agonizing and oh-so-mega-freaking typical. The story of my life really. My sister is a model while I walk dogs, my parental units are stuffy Anna-lovers, and even though I have a funny, popular, divinely gorgeous boyfriend, I have to pretend that I don't. If there's any Good Sense to be gleaned from this situation it's that nothing is ever perfect or turns out exactly like you hoped it would. Life is quite obviously about compromise—a give-and-take that requires grace and a whole lot of patience. You can never have it all your own way (unless you're Anna Watson, of course).

"I'm starving!" Pearl declares suddenly, ripping herself away from the computer screen and grinning wildly like a gambler on a winning streak. "Come on, there's cold pizza in the fridge."

It's just like Pearl to change a subject that isn't centered on her, I think to myself spitefully—even though I wasn't about to volunteer any further information about Toby and me anyway. It was nice of Frannie to ask though, and I divert my attention away from my thumbnail just long enough to give her a grateful smile. Fran's just about to disappear downstairs after Pearl when she suddenly turns around and lingers thoughtfully at the door.

"I had an appointment with my psychiatrist yesterday," she says. "I'm seeing her every fortnight now."

Fran doesn't often talk about what happened with Uncle Mannie, although I was aware that she was seeing a psychiatrist once a week. She must be getting better if she's only going every second week now.

"That's great Frannie," I reply sincerely. "Really great!"

"I saw Lucas there yesterday," she continues. "He was waiting to see one of the other psychiatrists."

"Oh, right," is all I can say. That doesn't seem strange, not now that I know about his bipolar disorder. But as much as I trust Frannie I can't very well tell her that. It's simply not mine to tell.

"Yeah well, small world, huh," Frannie

concludes with a smile. "You coming down for pizza?"

"I wouldn't mind checking my mail first," I respond. "You go ahead, I'll be down in a minute."

I wait for the sound of her footsteps on the stairs before I fire up Google and type "bipolar disorder" into the search box. I'm instantly faced with an endless list of sites and, as an ignorant novice on the subject, I simply click on the first one, which also just happens to have a government web address. I hope this makes it vaguely credible.

> Bipolar disorder, also known as manic-depressive illness, is a brain disorder that causes unusual shifts in a person's mood, energy, and ability to function. Different from the normal ups and downs that everyone goes through, the symptoms of bipolar disorder are severe.
>
> Bipolar disorder typically develops in late adolescence or early adulthood. It is often not recognized as an illness, and people may suffer for years before it is properly diagnosed and treated. It is a long-term illness that must be carefully

> managed throughout a person's life. It can be treated, and people with this illness can lead full and productive lives. Medications for bipolar disorder are prescribed by psychiatrists.

I read the information through twice and try to make the words correspond with my image of Lucas. On the outside he seems so cool and cavalier, and yet on the inside he's all churned up. I now feel very guilty about calling him Luc-Arse and I suddenly want to be his very best friend in the entire world. I'm sure I could fix him with great big Band-Aids of compassion and cheery encouragement. What I lack in information I'll make up for with enthusiasm! I'm so wrapped up in my conviction that for a millisecond I even forget about Toby. That hasn't happened for a while.

Chapter 14
Space Exploration

I've been in a mood this week, I can't lie. I decided that if Toby wants to play it cool, well, then I'm Miss North Pole. Of course I don't enjoy being quarrelsome one bit—it requires a lot of dedication and focus, but sometimes the situation requires it. That's not Good Sense logic, that's just a side-effect of being human.

I'm feeling seriously neglected these days, and it's taken over from any rational thoughts I might have been having (I say *might* because all these hormones make rational thought a bit of a hit and miss affair). I've started the third "Hearts and Flowers": *Race for Love*, but it hasn't helped to take my mind of my narkiness one bit. I've swapped Misty and Rick for Taylor and Sven, who is a racehorse trainer and a real meanie. Like Taylor says, he's the sort of bloke her mum warned her about. I'm not entirely sure that I know what she means by this—my own mum hasn't given me the same warning, but that's probably because she's too busy being an

Anna-lover. For all I know Toby could be crackers, not that anybody in my family would care. Today my self-pity is a dark, dank, bottomless pit.

Anna has another photo shoot later this afternoon so Mum has left work early again to help her prepare and ferry her to the studio. The convenience of the British public transport system is lost on them both, it seems. I'm sitting in our spare-room-slash-study and trying desperately to concentrate on writing an English essay on *Macbeth*, but Anna's bedroom is next door and it's almost impossible to think over the giggling. Mum is putting curlers in Anna's hair and for some reason they're both finding the experience side-splitting. Some people are too easily pleased.

"I'm trying to do my homework in here!" I finally holler in frustration. Sometimes I wonder why I even bother.

"Oh, Ella." Mum suddenly appears at the spare-room-slash-study door. "I forgot to mention that Norm's mate might stop by this afternoon to sort out that Internet thingamajig your dad's been going on about."

Internet thingamajig? High-tech Mum is not. And if it's a mate of Norm-from-the-pub then there's very little chance of him actually showing up when he says he will, but I gave up on enlightening this family a long time ago.

"Sure, I'll be here," I reply but don't take my eyes off the computer screen. Like I have anywhere to be . . . or anyone to see . . . or a life. I have *Macbeth*. The doorbell rings and Mum's voice is next door again.

"Could you get that, Ella?" These days Mum only acknowledges me when she needs me to do something.

"I'm busy with my homework!" I splutter furiously. They really are taking this too far.

The doorbells chimes a second time and this time I hear footsteps stomping down the stairs to the front door. This is followed by two sets of footsteps coming back up the stairs; Norm's mate must have kept his word. Imagine that! Mum is rattling on about Anna's modeling and curling her hair blah blah blah; I'm Cinderella—stuck at home without curly hair or a photo shoot to go to.

Anna's voice joins in the conversation and sounds serene and sophisticated. I'm not particularly interested in what she has to say, until I hear her speak the name "Toby." *Toby!* Here? It can't be. But I think it is. Noooo, I'm wearing my *Star Trek* pajamas.

"We shot the summer catalog a few weeks ago," Anna continues, "it was absolutely exhausting. Most of the shots involved me posing like this . . ."—the silence is perforated with muffled shuffling sounds—". . . but with different props each time, of course." She's actually modeling for him! I must stop her. But I mustn't let Toby see me dressed like this. "I can't tell you how difficult it is to make each shot look unique," she prattles on. "So what I do is I try to emphasize a different part of me each time. Like in one shot I might pose to highlight my cheekbones, and for the next I'll draw attention to my hips with my hands . . ."

Ugh! Just shoot me. *Now!* Suddenly, I'm standing right behind Toby. I think I made it from the chair in the spare-room-slash-study all the way to the door of Anna's bedroom without even touching the ground. Toby is scraping his hand through his hair with his shoulders curled, as if he's trying to make himself appear as small as possible. He looks distinctly uncomfortable.

I had planned to barge in and rescue him, but now that I see him squirming I'm suddenly in less of a hurry to interrupt the proceedings. I am, after all, suffering with bruised feelings . . . all his fault!

There's a saying that goes: "Hell has no fury like a woman scorned"; maybe I should update that to: "Don't get your girlfriend in a huff—you'd be amazed at how long she can carry a thing on for," and make it a Good Sense tip especially for blokes.

"Toby's come to visit." Mum has spotted me.

I can see that. "Hi Toby," I smirk, making it quite obvious that I was standing there all along. A few more minutes would have done it though.

"Hey Ellie," he exhales, looking visibly relieved, until he sees my *Star Trek* pajamas, that is. Ah yes, my pajamas. I'd forgotten about those. If the look on Toby's face is anything to go by, he's hoping he'll also forget about them . . . eventually, in time.

"Come on, we're going to be late," Mum clucks, shooing Anna and all her glittering accessories, lotions, and potions into a pile. I don't think Mum knows that Toby and I are an item (I'm not even sure if we are an item, come to think of it!), but I wonder if she'd be as happy to leave us alone if she did. I suppose there are some benefits to being ignored. Toby and I stand there looking awkward while Mum and Anna flit and flap and eventually swirl downstairs in a perfumed eddy of bags and trimmings.

"I came to tell you that we've got another job. Mr. Trent from the football club wants us to walk his Labrador, Duke," Toby finally reveals as the front door bangs shut.

Right. So that's it then? "Why didn't you just phone?" I sigh, giving it all the blasé I've got.

"Don't be like that, Ellie. I came to see you too, of course. You've been a bit odd this week and I wanted to make sure that you're okay."

"A bit odd"? Good grief, what does it take for you blokes to get the message—skywriting? Like Taylor says, men are all the same: they just have different faces so that you can tell them apart. But I don't say anything, and just bounce my shoulders uselessly.

"Nice pjs," Toby grins cheekily. "May the Force be with you!" I'm busy concocting a brilliantly snotty retort to this but I'm slow on the uptake and Toby is suddenly wrapping me up in his arms. "Come on, don't be angry with me, Ellie," he says, resting his chin on my head. His Adam's apple is pressing against my forehead and vibrating as he talks, which is creating a strangely pleasant buzzing sensation in my head. "I know it's a difficult situation, but we've all been mates for so long. We've just got to give ourselves and everybody else time to adjust."

"Doesn't mean you have to ignore me though, does it?" I grumble, or try to anyway—but my face is pressed up against his padded jacket, which is stifling my words.

"Pardon?"

"I said," I begin, pushing Toby gently away, "that you don't have to ignore me!"

"I wasn't ignoring you, but I also need some time with Tom-Tom and the others."

"I understand that, but *everything* has changed. I can't even do the things I used to do—when we were just best mates—any more, just in case somebody gets the wrong idea. Take that night at the theatre for example. Normally I would have bought you something to eat too but because we're now officially boyfriend and girlfriend—but pretending not to be some of the time but not all of the time—I have to think before I do anything!" That came out sounding very garbled, but I know what I meant.

"As usual you're analyzing everything too much," Toby replies, not in the least bit confused by my outburst. He really does know me better than anybody. I think I love him again.

"Just be yourself and I'll be me, that's all." And with that he squeezes me tightly and pulls me to his lips. I land with a blissful smack and instantly forget about everything in the entire universe apart from Toby Sinclair. He still tastes like marshmallows, just like the very first time we upside-down kissed in his bedroom in front of the CD player. And he still has the strongest arms in the world. This is where I am sheltered and warm and safe and loved. In heaven there are no seconds or minutes; we are oblivious to earthly intrusions like time and place. When Toby and I kiss we are our five senses, and nothing more. We connect through taste and touch, sound and smell. And we only have eyes for each other. In our private universe we are bright stars circling the fiery brilliance of a sun that is our blinding and eternal love. I've even forgotten about the gaudy jammies I'm wearing, until Toby slides his hands from my hips up and under the fleecy pajama top decorated with planets, spaceships, and strangely shaped aliens, that is.

His fingertips are warm and soft and rub small, sizzling patches on my belly. We've never done the hands-under-clothes thing before and I'm instantly anxious. I'm suddenly very aware of two things: the first is that he might feel my flab (it's too late to suck in now), and the second thing (in flashing neon!) is that we're just a few short stops away from my breasticles. And we've definitely never been there before. I can't focus on our kiss anymore; all I can think about is his fingertips blazing a trail along my skin which has suddenly set off a thousand goosebumps. I have been reduced to a midriff . . . a bumpy torso, and nothing more. The rest of me has melted away completely.

The circles Toby's fingertips trace on my belly arc wider and wider until they're practically brushing the edge of my ribcage. The feeling is exquisite and terrifying at the same time and I think I might be shaking—for both reasons. I don't know if I'm ready for the breasticle thing just yet, the only way to be sure is to see when it happens, but I don't know if I have the courage for that either. I think I'm probably going to have to inhale soon or risk passing out. Just when I think I might self-combust due to a lack of oxygen Toby suddenly changes tack and slides his hands from my front around to my breasticle-*less* back and locks me up in a snug hug. He then gently plucks his lips from mine and gazes down at me, grinning affectionately. The softness in his eyes makes my heart quiver and stall. I will love this boy forever.

Chapter 15
Public Relations

Duke the Labrador is thankfully everything Laika the bug-eyed gremlin is not. He's big and gold and so far poopy-free, and both Toby and I are thoroughly enjoying walking him through the park. We're like a wonderful family out for a stroll, marinating in the glorious springtime sunshine that's as dazzling as our moods. Things with our mates are going well and we seem to have found a balance between romance and friendship. Toby was right, everybody needs time to adjust—that's simply human nature.

I decide to take advantage of the moment and Toby's excellent advice and update him on Pearl's virtual boyfriend and the Pearlodrama that's no doubt lurking around the next corner. I wonder what he'll make of this Simon fellow.

"Seems unlikely," he responds once I've completed the abbreviated version of the story, "but then, of course, these days who knows."

That's it? I can hear the birds chirruping. This is too much like gossip for Toby, I should have known (although it's not like I overdosed on the details).

"She's planning on meeting up with him soon," I add, dangling one more juicy carrot.

"She'll find out for herself then, won't she?" Boys are no fun.

"Well, I certainly don't think he's a six-foot dreamboat with blue eyes, that's for sure," I state for the record. "That girl has got to take a vacation from Planet Pearl and visit Earth some time."

A man with a small black and white dog and a yellow tennis ball arrives at the park and Duke suddenly starts yanking on the lead. He wants to play ball or eat the other dog...or both—I don't know Duke well enough to be sure. Either way, it's put an end to our relaxing stroll.

"Let's head down Bluehouse Lane, it's nice and quiet there," Toby puffs, straining to keep a hold on Duke.

I nod in agreement and we both check the road for cars before crossing. I'm so busy keeping one eyeball on Duke and the other on the traffic I don't give a moment's thought to what might be waiting for us on the other side of road. Even if I had given it some thought, nothing could have prepared me for the jumbo poster of my twin sister simpering with a steaming Marks & Spencer baguette. She doesn't smile like that when she's at home.

Toby, Duke, and I come to a standstill beneath the poster and silently stare up at it for a few thoughtful moments.

"I think she's trying to emphasize her molars in this one," Toby quips, turning from the poster and grinning at me mischievously. Duke's interest is also fleeting and he quickly repositions himself and raises his leg against the wall below the poster. He may be poopy-free, but once he's finished Dunton could end up with its own Lake District. I hope I'm not expected to mop that lot up.

I think they're both being too critical. "Her eyes look lovely," I say, "and she seems very pleased with her freshly baked baguette, which really is the whole point of the poster, isn't it?" I only know that it's freshly baked because that's what it says right beside Anna's left ear, but then again it would have to be fresh for you to look that happy. So this is my sister's modeling debut, I reflect. I wonder if Anna realizes what she's let herself (and her relatives—me!) in for. Will life as we know it ever be the same again?

"Hey, Lucas." That was Toby's voice. I turn from the poster. And there's Lucas.

"Hiya," I greet him, but find nothing there. Lucas's eyes, usually so sparkling and lively, are drained and empty. Somebody has switched off his light. He looks from me to the poster, to me, to the poster, and back to me again. I feel like I'm watching Wimbledon.

"That you?" he asks immediately. So much for polite pleasantries then.

"No! Definitely, absolutely, categorically *not*!" I declare. "That's my twin sister. Her name is Anna. And we are two very different people." I wouldn't normally advertise Anna, but in this particular situation it really is the lesser of two evils. Lucas looks doubtful and Toby is laughing loudly. Even Duke has a big, toothy canine grin on him.

"It's true," Toby finally chuckles, sensing my swelling irritation. "I can vouch for the fact that Anna and Ella are two entirely different people. And that is not Ella. Nor is it her baguette, which is a pity. Ha ha."

"Just as well . . ." Lucas sniffs critically, "you'd have to be an arse to do that sort of thing."

"Oi, easy, Lucas—that's my sister you're talking about," I snap. It's quite obvious that something has changed Lucas, but his black mood doesn't give him the green light to abuse Anna. Just because you're angry or sad doesn't mean you have the right to make others feel that way too (that's some Good Sense Guide advice). Then I remember Lucas's bipolar disorder. Could it be responsible for transforming cheeky-cheery Lucas into the edgy, brooding stranger standing before me?

"Sorry," he finally shrugs, "but you didn't seem overly impressed with the poster either."

I must stop wearing my feelings on my face. "Yeah, well, she's still my sister," I mumble quietly, suddenly feeling bad for him. He looks like he's come undone; he might unravel completely if I push this any further.

"I didn't mean to insult her . . . or you," he continues. "I sometimes forget that people generally have feelings."

What's that supposed to mean? I wonder, but don't speak out loud. Right now I don't think I really do want to know what morose Lucas means. It's not the time and a busy street corner is not the place. Only ask the questions you genuinely want to hear the answers to, and this includes "How are you?" and "Do I look fat in this?" That's another one for the Good Sense Guide. I'm on fire today; I obviously think well under pressure.

"It's cool," I say simply. The three of us stand there staring awkwardly at each other and the ground while Duke tugs at his lead and sniffs out things he hasn't yet marked as his territory. This dog's bladder is bottomless.

"Okay, *ciao* then," Lucas suddenly drawls, does an about-turn and strides off quickly down the road, overtaking pedestrians while his trailing rusty curls struggle to keep up. He didn't even give us the chance to say good-bye.

I contemplate telling Toby about his bipolar disorder, but then decide against it, figuring that this really is Lucas's secret to tell. I don't normally keep anything from Toby, but in this case I don't think he'd mind. We understand and trust each other's motives; that's what makes us a star couple.

Chapter 16
Web of Deceit

I am being forced to run around and chase a basketball with the rest of my classmates. The only good news of the day is that we're doing this running and chasing in the gym, which is indoors. I don't see why we don't just play netball, seeing as we're all familiar with the sport, but Miss Hurst—the PE teacher—likes to "keep things interesting." She's fresh out of teacher-training college and still has too much enthusiasm for her own good. Or *our* good, I should say. I'm taking as long as I can to warm up; the more stretching we do the less basketball we play. Pearl is right beside me, hopping about like a kangaroo and drawing attention to herself as usual.

"What are you so happy about?" I grumble, desperately trying to touch my toes. Ugh, I think I've gone cross-eyed.

"Simon mailed me last night, we're meeting up this afternoon!" she sings gleefully, squeezing out a little, high-pitched squeal at the end.

So today is the day Precious Pearl and Buff

Bloke finally set their starry eyes on each other. This should be interesting. "What's the plan then?" I wheeze, wishing I had shorter legs or longer trainers.

"He's picking me up from the park at four," Pearl replies, "and then we're going to find somewhere nice to have a romantic bite to eat."

"Which park, the one near your house?" Just a few more inches . . .

"No, the one on the way to Eppingworth, you know—with the statue of Walter Churchill," she explains and reaches lithely for the ground.

"It's Winston Churchill," I correct her, "and that's miles from anywhere! Crikey Pearl, you don't even know him. Why don't you at least meet up at a public place? The Pisces Café in the high street does perfectly good fish and chips." Where is Frannie when you need her? She'd be able to talk some sense into this crazy girl.

"There you go again." Pearl sighs, rolling her eyeballs to the back of her head. "You should join the drama club, Ella Mental, because you really do know how to make a production out of everything. He's not some blimmin' monster or a convict. He's picking me up in a flashy Merc, you know. Do you really think freakazoids drive

Mercedes? I don't think so." The last sentence spins out of her mouth in a patronizing singsong. How do I argue with that sort of twisted logic? I guess I don't.

"Oh, whatever Pearl. . . ." I sigh and also abandon touching my toes. I'm going to have to get some help with this particular Pearlodrama. And as for my toes, well I never needed to touch them anyway.

I survive basketball and eventually find Fran packing up ready to head home. It doesn't take me long to fill her in on the most recent developments in Pearl's cyber love life.

"William Churchill Park?" she muses thoughtfully. "Isn't that near the Hog and Hound?"

"No, it's near Eppingworth, which is the middle of nowhere," I reveal. "And it's Winston Churchill, by the way."

"Ah, right," she replies. "And?"

"And I think we should spy on them and make sure that everything goes okay." Maybe I'm right, maybe I'm just plain Ella Mental—but the Good Sense Guide says better safe than sorry.

"And if it doesn't?" Fran asks. Her mouth is straight but her eyes are curled up in amusement.

"Well, I bloody don't know!" I snap irritably.

"She's your friend too. And besides, I just don't trust this Buff Bloke character. I guess I have a funny feeling about the whole thing." It's all come together too smoothly, and if I've learned anything, it's that real life rarely goes this smoothly. But I don't update Frannie on this nugget of insight; she already thinks I'm overcooked.

Fran finally agrees to my plan and we stop off at her house to drop our bags off and eat before heading out to catch a bus that will take us to Churchill Park. Although she doesn't come right out and say it, I get the impression that Fran is doing this for me instead of Pearl. Not because she doesn't care about Pearl, but because she thinks she's indulging my cuckoo imagination.

Winston Churchill Park is basically a large triangle-shape of green grass situated between a disused farm stall, some grazing fields, and a trickle of a river. Only a very small portion of the park ground is actually bordered by the road, which is good news. Simon will be using the road to collect Pearl, which means that not only are we guaranteed of being in the right place at the right time, but we can also keep a much closer eye on the proceedings.

By the time we finally reach the park it's almost ten to four and I'm terrified that Pearl has beaten us there. She'd burst a blood vessel if she knew what we were up to! But luckily we have just enough time to strategically select a bush that's growing two meters from a solitary park bench, which is about three meters from the road. This means that we'll be hidden from sight but close enough to give this Simon a once-over.

Pearl arrives a few minutes after we've safely concealed ourselves in the leafy camouflage and takes a seat on the bench, swiftly adjusting her skirt and preening herself excitedly. I glance over at Fran for reassurance. It doesn't take a mastermind to see that she's on the verge of wetting herself with bottled-up laughter. That, or she's having a fit, but either way her chest is pulsing, her eyes are wet and creased, and the hand clamped to the lower half of her face is the only thing stopping her muffled mirth from leaking out all over the place.

"Don't you dare!" I mouth voicelessly. Fran gives me a reassuring thumbs-up gesture with one hand, but doesn't risk removing the other hand from her still-grinning jaws. I'm definitely maturing quicker than my friends. After what feels like an idle age a Mercedes finally noses its way around the bend and slowly sputters up the road toward us. And even though this is nothing unexpected, my heart begins throbbing with the anticipation of what may or may not happen. Simon was spot-on about driving a Mercedes, although this particular Mercedes appears to be rather ancient and entirely flash-*less*. Still, we shouldn't judge him on his car.

Pearl spies the Merc the same moment we do; I can tell by the way she suddenly sits up straight and tilts her head coyly to one side. With the car no less than a few meters away she appears unable to contain her excitement any longer and jumps up and anxiously starts skipping from one foot to the other. The car sidles up to the curb and eventually comes to a standstill in front of the bench and Pearl. That's no eighteen year old. The driver is an aging man with a puffy, lined face stained orange with fake tan. His dark hair is seasoned with gray and thinning on top, but he otherwise appears to be rather unremarkable and not someone you'd take much notice of. Pearl solidifies at the sight of him but maintains her ground.

"Hey, you must be Precious Pearl," he greets her cheerily like some long-lost friend. Pearl doesn't answer so Mr. Fake-Tan continues talking. "Simon has told me all about you, sweetheart. And he's so sorry he's not here to pick you up himself. His wheels aren't quite ready yet and he's still stuck at the garage. Ha, these mechanics are a finicky lot! Ha ha. Anyway, he didn't want to keep you waiting so he asked me to fetch you and take you back to the garage. He said to tell you that he'd make it up to you with the best grub you ever tasted." Mr. Fake-Tan finally stops talking but continues beaming a smile at Pearl.

"Er, I don't know . . ." Pearl finally mutters. "Who did you say you were?"

"Oh, where are my manners?" Mr. Fake-Tan snickers. "I'm Jimmy, and I'm Simon's mate from the garage . . . been doing his family's cars since Simon was knee-high to a grasshopper. Ha, cute fella, that Simon. And he's nuts about you! Precious Pearl this and Precious Pearl that, it's all he's been talking about."

Pearl is munching on her top lip and shepherding her thoughts into some kind of order. "Okay. Fine, all right then," she finally agrees, arcing her way toward the passenger side of the car. I gaze in dismay at Fran, who is no longer laughing and now looks equally horrified.

"Pearl, do not get in the car!" I suddenly yell, springing from the bushes and stumbling forward a few paces. I have twigs caught in my hair and there's blood where a thorn has dug its groove in my arm, but I don't care one bit. "You're making a big mistake. There is no Simon!" I shout frantically.

Pearl swings around, her face contorting with surprise and fear. "Whaaat . . . ?" she yelps.

Shock turns Jimmy Fake-Tan's orange flesh a sallow shade of worm skin, but he remains doggedly perched behind the wheel of his car. "Just get in, sweetheart," he grins uneasily. "I haven't got time to play childish games. Neither has Simon."

Like someone has switched on the floodlights, Pearl's face instantly illuminates with the reality of the situation and her expression transforms from one of panic into steely determination. "You tell Simon I'll be waiting right here," she commands Jimmy Fake-Tan, "because I don't think I'll be going with you, grandpa!"

The smile on Jimmy Fake-Tan's face flips upside down to form an angry sneer and his knuckles pale with the strain of gripping the steering wheel. "You can go to hell, sweetheart!" he spits bitterly, his face twisting with malicious rage. Tiny beads of sweat have broken out on his forehead like blistering paintwork and he looks ready to kill. "Just who do you think you are way, huh? Little tramps like you get what they deserve!" With that parting shot he jams the accelerator pedal and disappears down the road in a screech of tires. Soon all that's left of Jimmy Fake-Tan's battered Mercedes is the rancid smell of burning rubber and a wispy plume of gray smoke.

Pearl, Fran, and I remain motionless in its wake, each bleary with fear and wide-eyed with jubilation. It takes a while for us to breathe again, and our first synchronized gasp of air is deep and rasping. Pearl is still trying to make some sense of what just happened. Her pale neck is mottled with blood-red splotches while her round eyes ricochet off us like pent up rubber balls. We're just as shaken by our narrow escape and only a little less surprised. This could have ended so differently, and for the first time ever our Internet heroine appears meek and as close to thankful for her friends as I think she'll ever be. Pearl's marvelous romance came within touching distance of an unforgettable tragedy.

I think I've just settled on Good Sense Guide number thirty-nine: Things that seem too good to be true usually aren't true at all.

Chapter 17
Banana Split

Fran and I have just finished giving statements to two very nice policewomen called Margaret and Eileen. Both were really friendly and attentive and more like sympathetic aunties than packing law-enforcement officers. I could have nattered for hours. I don't often get people hanging off my every word and although they said that Fran and I should have gone to our parents instead of tracking Pearl, they thought we were mature and thoughtful young people.

Pearl spent over four hours with Margie and Eileen and finally emerged from the principal's office looking superstar-smug, like she'd just been interviewed for *CosmoGIRL!* or something. If I was expecting her to be grateful or downcast about the Jimmy Fake-Tan incident I was wrong. She's as loud and brazen as ever. She's been beating on everyone's eardrum, telling them how she narrowly escaped the "greasy clutches of some cyber freak." I think the word is *saved* rather than *escaped*, but as usual Pearl has interpreted reality with her own brand of crazy. The seriousness of the situation seems to have been lost on her, which probably means that she hasn't learned her lesson. Still, if any good comes out of her big-mouth blabbing it's that everyone else will realize that anybody can use Internet chat rooms, sleazy orange creepos too. These days you've got to be smart (which I obviously *am not*—not if I was expecting any gratitude from Pearl!).

I arrive home and slam the front door behind me in frustration. The loud bang is very satisfying; a voice for my bottlenecked irritation. Anna is on the couch and reading a book, or she was until I slammed the door. Now she's holding the book to her chest. I don't think I've ever seen Anna read a book before. That's what a day at home with a cold will do for you.

"Must you slam doors; you nearly gave me a heart attack!" she shrieks dramatically.

"I doubt it," I mumble, and ditch my school bag. I'm starving.

Anna's gone diva on me and is now using the book to fan her face while she drinks down deep breaths of air. Oh, please. I'm about to cut her a large slice of my mind when I suddenly recognize the illustrated cover of the book she's using to fan her mug. It's *Race for Love.* I'd know Sven and Taylor anywhere.

"Where did you find that?" I shout, pointing at the book with my eyeballs out on stalks.

"In your bedroom," Anna replies, trying to plaster over her guilt with nonchalance. "I was looking for...uh, my shoo...coat."

"Your *shoocoat*?" I repeat slowly. "Don't think I've ever heard of one of those before. That a new accessory then?" I'm circling Anna with shark-like stealth. The last time I was this angry I passed cranberry juice through my nose.

"My coat! I was looking for my beige coat with the belt," Anna huffs indignantly, like people do when they're lying, "and I came across this book. And you know how I love books."

"You were snooping in my room!" I yell. "Wait until I tell Mum..."

"So Mum knows you're reading this then?' Anna butts in and flourishes the book tauntingly. Indignation has mutated into a self-satisfied smirk.

"Er . . . 'course she does." I decide to chance it.

Like the sun rising at dawn, Anna's face slowly illuminates with a know-it-all grin. The books are old and tatty and don't have a library mark on them; one plus one equal two. "You nicked these from Mum, didn't you!" she roars triumphantly, like she just solved one of life's biggest mysteries. "I remember seeing some old paperbacks in Mum's cupboard, although I wasn't particularly interested in them. Ha, if only I'd known."

"Oh, I thought you loved books?"

"'Hearts and Flowers,' yah-haaa!" Anna bobs her head enthusiastically.

"You still shouldn't have been snooping in my room, Anna Watson."

"And you shouldn't have been snooping in Mum's cupboard, Ella Watson."

"But so have you!" I whine. This conversation doesn't seem to be going anywhere.

"That Sven's a corker," Anna chortles. "Did you nick this for reference material then?" She's jiggling her eyebrows saucily and waving *Race for Love* in the air.

"I didn't nick it, I borrowed it." I squirm. "And why don't you keep your rump out of my business?"

Anna pulls a face at me but has the sense to change the subject. Toby and I weren't of *that* much interest to her anyway. "The parental units are pretty upset about the whole Internet loony thing, by the way."

"I spent an hour with them in the principal's

office this morning," I groan. "Tell me something I don't know." Toby's also uppity with me, calling me soft in the head and wanting to know why I didn't ask him instead of Fran to go to Churchill Park, nag-nagity-nag. Which is all well and good, but had I gone to him he probably would have told me to stay out of it. And had I gone to the units I know they would have told me to tell Pearl's mum or something just as unhelpful. Not even I *really and truly* thought that this Simon would be dangerous. Hindsight is an exact science. And that isn't from the Good Sense Guide; it just means that it's easy to be a know-it-all when something has already happened!

"Mum phoned and said Dad wants to have a family meeting later," Anna continues. "I only hope this stupid business hasn't jeopardized our chances of getting the Internet at home."

I twist from the telly to face my self-centered sibling. My lower jaw has come loose. "Is that all you can think about?" I ask, dumbfounded. "Are you really that selfish?"

"I'm thinking about all of us, aren't I? We've all been looking forward to getting the Internet, not just me." She's inspecting her fingernails like they belong in the National Gallery.

"Oh geez, Anna," I seethe, "to think I was shoved up against you in a womb for nine long months. Thank Frank none of you rubbed off on me. You really are too freaking much!" I signal the end of conversation by reclaiming *Race for Love* and stomping off in the direction of the kitchen. There is no Frank; I was just caught up in the moment.

I'm concentrating on pretending I'm adopted while I cut slices of banana for a mashed-banana sandwich when I hear the front door open and voices that are louder and different to the ones in my head. Now the door is closing and a new voice is nattering. The parental units are home early and have already zoned in on Anna. Brilliant. I have a sudden urge to stab myself in the eye with the rest of this banana.

"ELLA!"

That's my summons from Dad then. How I wish this family would get into the habit of walking and talking; this standing and hollering is completely Neanderthal. My mashed-banana sandwich and I find the units with Anna in the living room. "Yes?"

"Plate?" Mum sighs.

There's a lull while I amble back to the kitchen and locate a plate to contain the crumbs that may or may not have sprinkled from my lunch onto the carpet. I return with my sandwich and a plate but don't say anything because I have a mouth full of banana and bread.

"Your dad wants to have a family meeting," Mum says.

I don't swallow because that'll mean I'll have to reply so I just keep on chewing.

"You already know how concerned your mother and I are about what you and Fran did yesterday, so I won't harp back to it. You put yourselves in a very dangerous situation. Even if your hearts were in the right place, I will expect you girls to start thinking with your heads from now on. Are we clear?" Chew. Nod. Chew. I now have a banana-sandwich milkshake in my mouth. "I have decided that we will still get the Internet at home, but I don't want any of this chat room business going on. Norm's mate is going to set up parental controls so that you girls have limited access to websites." Parental control is to my father what double-chocolate is to the rest of the free world. "Are we clear?"

I'm now starting to feel nauseous and am going to have to swallow the banana-bread mush or risk losing it in the other direction. "Crystal clear," I finally gulp. And we needed a family meeting for that?

"I just don't understand why you didn't come to us in the first place," Mum finally speaks. Normally I would expect this to sound like a stern statement, but today her voice is soft and her eyes are tapered and pleading. Now she wants to talk to me?

"Yes, and there's that too," Dad adds uncomfortably, determined to continue presiding over this conversation.

Are they being serious? "Well, let's see, could it be because nobody in this family has any time or interest in me, apart from Anna who enjoys dressing me up like Streetwalker Barbie? Or might the fact that my name is the punchline for this family's jokes have something to do with it? And how about if you tried listening once in a while, instead of constantly shouting out orders and rules all the time? Then I just might have discussed Pearl with you."

"Streetwalker Barbie?!" Anna squawks. She's only interested in the bits that involve her and the fact that I'm aiming a blow for justice—

justice she might benefit from—is completely lost on her.

"Come on, that's not true at all," Mum says, but her tone is offhand and sounds more like a conclusion than a discussion. I think she's hoping I'll lose interest and just drop the subject like I usually do. But not this time!

"Course it is," I sulk. "You're always out shopping for Anna and flapping over her modeling career. You haven't even asked me how my dog-walking is going." I really wish I hadn't had to say that. "As for you," I turn to face Dad, "all you ever do is fork out more rules. And there's some serious favoritism going on in this family, which is fine—but then don't suddenly start wondering why I don't confide in you."

Anna and the units stare at me without speaking, which doesn't happen often. I don't usually blab my mind and I think they're all a little shocked by the eruption. I'm shocked too, if the truth be told. And because I've never really done this before I'm now also unsure as to what I should do next. I cross my arms in an attempt to appear stern but just feel like a kid in a strop. I must also look rather silly with a sandwich sticking out of my right hand, so I untangle my arms and take a haughty bite of my mashed-banana sandwich instead. As I stand there defiantly chewing for all I'm worth the only sound I can hear above the gobsmacked silence is banana and bread churning around and around in my mouth. I'm sure the three of them can hear it too. If I had a plan, this would not be it.

Suddenly the sound of my chewing is replaced by the shrill ring of a mobile phone. It rings three times before I realize that it's coming from my blazer pocket. "Excuse me, I have a call," I mumble through sandwich, and turn to leave the room. Not only do I have a call, but I also have caller ID, which is telling me that my hero has come to save me. I manage to swallow before I press the green button. "Hi, Tobes!"

He wants to know if I'm okay. He says he hopes I'm not out and about chasing loonies again. He's wondering if he should come over. He even asks if I'd like to chat about anything. My boyfriend is cluck-clucking over me and being so protective and feeling guilty for being a non-communicator. I am seriously loved!

"Ella?" Mum is in the kitchen standing behind me.

I finish saying good-bye to Toby and press the

red button on my mobile before I turn to face her. "Uh-huh?"

"You may be right about what you said," she begins, "and I want you to know that we're all really very sorry."

I don't remember the units using the sorry word before and I'm tempted to ask for it in writing. Still, the Good Sense Guide says that it takes a big person to apologize, so I'll resist the temptation.

"It's okay." I finally nod and manage a smile. "And uh, thanks. I suppose I still should have told you about it, it was stupid not to. Anyway, Toby and I are going to the funfair this weekend." And with that parting statement and a very wide grin, I gallop up the stairs to my bedroom.

Chapter 18
Fair Game

H'lo Peeps,

'Tis me again, the Tin Man still looking for his heart. Not much has changed since my last posting, although I've written a couple of songs. One of them is called "Running on Empty," and it's about spending your life trying to escape the emptiness and loneliness inside you. I've got to leave this place! I don't belong here. Maybe I'll go sing with the angels instead.

S'long,

TM

This message was posted on PPT three days ago. I scroll back through the past few weeks' messages, wondering if Tin Man has left anything else. I'm strangely intrigued by this person I know almost nothing about. I'm presuming Tin Man is a boy, and I think what fascinates me most about him is the fact that he seems so desperate to showcase his soul and the cogs and wheels that make him tick. He's turned himself inside out and put his heart and guts on display, and yet left us to imagine the rest of him—like who he is and what he looks like. Anonymity is a great tongue-greaser.

The only other message from Tin Man is a curt and rather obnoxious reply to someone else's posting. He thinks Spaceboy is a "moronic muppet" for reporting bullying to his teacher. Spaceboy has retaliated and called him an "opinionated fathead." I somehow don't think that this is what Tom-Tom had in mind when he created Pinboard Psychology for Teens.

"When do I get a chance, crazy girl?"

There's a new reflection in the computer screen. Ah, the lovely Anna Watson. "My hour isn't up yet," I yap.

"Yeah, well, almost! And I hope that isn't a chat room site you're on."

"No, it isn't. And what I do in my hour is none of your business, either." I'm pretty sure Tom-Tom's website doesn't qualify.

The parental units' newfound guilt got us the Internet much sooner than anticipated, and without any further orders or lectures either. Dad's walking around looking like he's suffering from chronic indigestion, but so far he's managed to board up his overwhelming urge to dominate with a silent, feeble smile. As Anna's reflection withdraws from the computer screen I guide my thoughts back to Tin Man. I find his most recent posting again, hit the "reply to message" icon below and begin typing.

Dear Tin Man,

I don't know you or what's going on to make you sound so down, but the one thing I have learned is that no matter what happens or how bad it seems today, life does go on, and it will get better. You shouldn't be talking about singing with the angels. Sometimes I find it helps to remember that you're not alone. Sure, your problems may be your own, but everyone has problems. One of my best friends just had the hardest time you can imagine, something that went all the way back to her childhood. You should talk to someone, like she did. Remember, a good angle to approach any problem is a try-angle. Good luck and keep your dial tuned to a smile. Lilac Laserin x

I'm tempted to tell him more about Frannie, just to prove that there are other teenagers out there with problems so heavy they could easily grind your bones to fine white dust, but of course I don't—I'd never betray Fran. I read my mail through once more before pressing the "send" button. It's brimming with good sense logic, and I scribble down some notes to transfer to my diary with the Good Sense Guide growing inside while it's all still warm and fragrant in my mind.

Lilac Laserin is an anagram of Ella Sinclair, which is what I'll be called when Toby and I get married. Of course I realize that this won't happen for a few years yet but I'm eager to try it out, and this is the next best thing. Just typing it makes my insides fizz with joy. Plus I really like the name Lilac; it's bags better than Ella. I think I may call our first daughter Lilac.

Anna is back. "Are you done yet!" That wasn't a question.

I quickly click the red cross at the top right corner and watch as the webpage rapidly sucks itself up into a tiny square in the center of the screen before disappearing completely. "Yes, Anna, I'm done. Are you happy now." That wasn't a question either and I gather up my things and stride from the spare-room-slash-study to my bedroom. Toby will be here in an hour to take me to the funfair anyway, but I don't tell Anna this. The units have ordered her to be nice to me (and no more dressing me up like Streetwalker Barbie), but her goodwill lasted all of fifteen minutes. And that was only because she wanted to borrow my math homework. At least no one has referred to my dog-walking enterprise again, thank goodness. That's more like toilet duty.

The sights are as loud as the sounds filling every nook and cranny of my ears. Everywhere you look there are vivid shades of every color imaginable. Red and yellow toy cars and speedboats glide on invisible tracks; a not-so-big Big Wheel turns in pinks and purples; stallions gallop in coats of white and chocolate decorated with bold metallic swirls; booths in green, blue and black hold contrasting signboards high; and flat-topped roofs with tassels of light bulbs burn as bright and orange as the tangerine slush in Mr. Fruity's slowly churning blender.

The sound of shouting and laughter and jumpy organ music plays out over the seamless background drone of engines whirring, humming and buzzing. And nothing remains still, not even for a millisecond. People are strolling or jostling determinedly; machines are spinning and jigging and shaking from side to side; even the mushroom sky is swirling and tempting the blueness beyond with the promise of a cameo appearance. Tom, Fran, Toby, and I are milling about the funfair entrance waiting for Lucas and Pearl, who are twenty minutes late. We were waiting in the queue, until we got to the front, that is.

"We should have told Pearl to meet us here an hour earlier, that way she'd probably be here on time," Fran sighs, sniffing the hot dogs wafting past her in the air.

"Here they come," I announce, catching Pearl's ivory hair and Lucas's long strides pushing through the crowds. We automatically rejoin the queue and by the time Lucas, Pearl, and her breasticles reach us we've shuffled halfway to the front already.

"Nice top!" Tom-Tom cheekily comments. Pearl is wearing a red low-cut top that practically plummets to her belly button. Not only is it low-cut, but it's also very tight and clings to her curves like hot sauce on ice cream. I glance over at Toby to give him a *what-is-she-like* roll of my eyeballs and notice that his gaze is also glued to her chest. I think he may even be drooling. My rosy little world suddenly turns an unsettling shade of green.

"So sorry we're late." Pearl smiles like this is a beauty pageant and all she wants is world peace. She doesn't offer any explanation for her tardiness though.

"I'll pay for you, shall I?" Lucas asks without looking up from her breasticles. Does he honestly expect them to answer?

"Thanks, Lukey," she replies, fluffing her hair and smoothing down her blouse. Any lower and she's committing a felony, I think to myself spitefully. Where's a policeman when you need one? Probably harassing some poor dog-walker about pavement poopy, no doubt!

I know Pearl is my friend, which makes my next thought super-size bitchy, but I really expected Toby to have a little more class. Look at him, darting sneaky glances at her you-know-whats (if I say it I'll detonate)! Pearl is blissfully aware of the attention her exposed cleavage is receiving but pretending to be quite oblivious to the fuss.

"Come on, it's our turn," Fran suddenly announces with a shake of her head. And she's right; we've all been so absorbed by Pearl's girlie bits we haven't even noticed the queue moving.

Toby waits his turn and then stoops to address the woman taking admission fees. "Two tickets, please," he says, and slides a tenner in her direction.

"I can pay for myself!" I blurt out, and jostle him two inches to the right with my elbow. I slap three pound coins down on the counter like a bookie with a bet and stare balefully at the woman behind the screen. She responds with a sigh and a look that straddles the fence between uncertainty and irritation.

"Don't be daft, Ella," barks Toby.

"Take my money, please!" I order the woman who has now jumped off the fence and landed squarely on the side of irritation. She glares at us silently for a few ticks of the clock above her head before accepting my coins as well as Toby's tenner.

"That's thirteen quid you've given me and seven quid change I'm giving you back," she says, and lobs a large handful of fifty-pence coins down on the counter in front of us. "Now sort it out between yourselves." She smiles, relishing the fact that we're now going to be jangling with pockets heavy with metal. Well, one of us will; it's not my change.

I turn from the counter and stretch my legs to catch up with Frannie, leaving Toby free to stare at Pearl's breasticles at his leisure. One push-up bra and these blokes are mush. It's worrying how much power two fleshy bumps can wield. And as for Pearl, well I don't even know why I'm surprised any more. I sneak a quick peek at my own breasticles and get a clear view right down to my feet. My strength is my mind, I reassure myself. And I have really good hand-eye coordination. *Hardly the same thing as large, pert breasticles though, is it*, my cynical side grumbles.

"Look, a Shoot 'n' Win stall, and they have some fab prizes!" Fran points out.

I trace her outstretched hand and land on the row of large, black-eyed, stuffed panda bears suspended from the stall's ceiling. *Yeah, but they're hardly large, pert breasticles, are they?* the same cynical voice in my head mutters (even though I think it might be time to move on). "Let's have a go then." I attempt a smile.

The spongy man in the cable-knit jersey manning the Shoot 'n' Win stall sniffs out our interest and immediately launches into his sales pitch with great gusto and expansive arm gestures that could bring in a Boeing. "You shoot and you win," he blares. "All you have to do is aim three Velcro balls at the target and score more than twenty-one points to receive a prize. Sounds simple, but you'll be surprised at how addictive it is!" He proffers a small, blue ball hopefully and continues grinning at us.

"Right, I'll have a go then," I reply, and accept the scratchy ball. I take a moment to focus on the target and then winch my arm back for momentum, when suddenly the ball disappears from my grip.

"Allow me, my lady," says Toby, who now just happens to be holding my ball. "One panda coming up!"

Normally this would have me chugging like a steam train; today I'm resisting the urge. But I don't argue either and even take a step back to allow Toby to swagger theatrically in front of the target. He turns to give me one final seductive wink before skillfully launching the blue ball at the black rings that look like ripples on the round fuzzy board. Eight points. He plucks the second ball from Twinkie Man's grasp and aims a second time. Five points. This might turn out to be a lesson in humility, I muse. The third ball takes flight and sticks to the ten-point ring. I should have known; Toby is good at everything. Everybody cheers, except Pearl—who is too busy looking cool, and me—because well, I'm too busy sulking.

"Your panda, my lady," Toby delivers the stuffed toy with a proud flourish and seals the deal with an *I-know-I'm-not-perfect-but-boy-aren't-I-lovable* wonky sort of grin. Behind the smile and higher up in his eyes I can see that he's sorry for whatever he did to annoy me (even though he's not entirely sure what it was), and I feel myself defrosting.

"Er, thanks." I smile and accept the toy. I suppose I was acting like a bit of a bunny boiler. With Shoot 'n' Win defeated we all amble on to the next attraction with Lucas and Tom-Tom leading the way, both boys now equally determined to prove themselves the first chance they get.

"Don't be mad at me, Ellie," Toby says, taking my hand.

"Yeah, well don't ogle Pearl's breasticles then!"

"Why would I?" He grins mischievously. "Yours are much nicer."

Uh, right. We've never really discussed breasticles and other sex thingies before and my body suddenly goes into emergency shut-down so that my brain can focus on making sense of this next phase in our relationship. All I can do is stand there with my jaws flapping in the breeze while my head gets a grip.

"They're nicer?" I finally gulp.

"Oh, yes siree!" Toby grins and hooks his arm around my neck in a playful headlock. Course they are, I grin back and make a dent in my back so that my front pushes out. I've heard about girl power, and now I think I might finally understand what it's all about.

Up ahead the rest of our group have come to a standstill and are crowding whatever it is that's seized their interest. Toby and I join their ranks, peering in to get a look. It's a large glass box with a scalloped red-and-white canvas roof, and trapped inside is the sleeping head and torso of what looks exactly like an old gypsy woman, but on closer inspection turns out to be a life-size and startlingly realistic dummy of an old gypsy woman. If the large hoop earrings, black bun, and embroidered dress and shawl leave any space for doubt, the crystal ball in front of her certainly brings it home. I don't notice the red curly painting on the glass until I step closer. It reads:

Gypsy Grandma Fortune Teller

I push my nose against the polished glass: her skin seems to be made out of some sort of rubber that's dark and lined and eerily lifelike. I'm very glad her eyes are closed. Even her textured clothing looks like it belongs to a real person (who obviously doesn't need them any more so may now be dead). The entire contraption looks ancient and very creepy and I'd like to vacate the spot right away, but everybody else is intrigued and prattling on like mad hatters at a tea party.

"This is the one for me!" Lucas announces as he searches for the coin slot, which is just below a neat square of pinprick holes and a glossy engraved plaque that reads:

Insert 2 x £1 coins and speak clearly
into the microphone so that Gypsy
Grandma can answer your question.

Lucas is shiny with enthusiasm and wastes no time feeding the old woman's belly with his coins. Nothing happens for what feels like minutes and just as we're about to get annoyed, Gypsy Grandma moves. Her chest starts heaving as if she's breathing air, her head tilts slightly to one side, and her eyes snap open. They're so dark they're almost black. She blinks twice before slowly shifting her hand over the crystal ball, and even though her movements have a robotic shudder to them—like they're being guided by a grid—the whole effect is freak-out fabulous! Of course we've all seen movies and played video games featuring the most incredible hi-tech animatronics and special effects known to modern man, but nothing—absolutely nothing—could touch the vision of this old woman breathing and blinking inside her glass-walled prison. I can't help wondering what it smells like in there.

"Ask her your question!" Pearl hisses.

Lucas's Adam's apple is pulsing in his neck but he otherwise appears calm. He grinds a path clear in his throat first and then finally asks, "Will I ever be famous?"

Under any other circumstances I'm quite sure we'd have mocked him silly for asking this particular question, but right now we're too caught up in the bizarreness of the moment. Gypsy Grandma's chest continues heaving and her eyes blink once more as her hand trembles ever so slightly over the crystal ball. Nothing. And then suddenly two things happen: a yellow light starts flashing close to Lucas's knee, and Gypsy Grandma falls instantly back into a deep sleep.

Pearl drops with her nose to the flashing yellow light and then returns to her full height with a small white card in her grip. "'People near and far will talk and write about you for a long time to come,'" she reads, and then gazes up at Lucas as if he were made out of eighteen-carat gold. "Nooooo way!" Now she's squealing. I must admit that I'm just as impressed.

"That's wicked, man!" Tom-Tom grins.

"Incredible! Completely unbelievable," Frannie bubbles over. The only one silent is Toby.

"So what do you think?" I ask breathlessly.

"There certainly was some skill involved in making that thing," he replies with a casual nod.

"Aw, come on, that was brilliant," I reply. "Let's give it a go." I want to ask if I'll ever be the real Lilac Laserin.

"No way." Toby shrugs.

"Come on," I whine.

"Don't fancy it."

"Please?"

"Uh uh." Toby shakes his head.

I suppose I could have my own private chat with Gypsy Grandma, but she freaks me out too much. "Very pretty please?"

"I'm hungry," Toby announces. "You think they sell shish kebabs around here? That's just what I feel like."

"Is that all you can think about?" I brood. Toby's definitely a facts kind of guy while I'm obviously more of a fiction kind of girl. I suppose nothing is going to change that, not even Mrs. Lilac Laserin.

Chapter 19

Saved by the Bell

Anna and I are breaking from tradition and voluntarily spending some time together. Well, I say voluntarily—but under extenuating circumstances. The female unit has joined a book club and right now there's a group of strange (and I don't mean as in I've never met them before) women perched on our sofa drinking wine spritzers. They began the book-club proceedings with a pyramid of books weighing down the coffee table in the living room, but it wasn't long before most of these "must-reads" had been relegated to the carpet to make room for more wine, chip 'n' dip, and an isolated and almost-full bottle of soda.

The male unit has gone fishing with Norm-from-the-pub and won't be home until tomorrow, and our mother looks like she's found her "on" switch. Unfortunately Anna and I are not benefiting from the situation; the telly is in the living room. Worse still, if we want food it looks like we're going to have to forage for it ourselves. It's only when I finally stride into the living room and openly announce that I'm making glorious quantities of cinnamon pancakes with fruit smoothies that Mum shoves a couple of ATM-crisp notes in my hand and mouths the words *Pizza Express* at us. Mrs. Jankowski has just started telling the rest of the ladies about Mr. Jankowski's vasectomy, so Anna and I really don't need to be told twice. We've grabbed our phones and are out the front door before you can say "painful burning sensation."

The late-afternoon light is soft and warm. Mother Earth has finally shifted and repositioned herself to give the northern hemisphere a better view of the sun and Dunton is stretched out and basking in the sunshine. The bare, skinny limbs of trees are growing fatter with pregnant buds that are photosynthesizing luxuriously in the sunlight, and the warmth is sucking at the boggy soil and drying out the mushy grass so that it's almost as smooth as felt and easy to walk on. We can cut eight minutes off our walk to the Pizza Express if we take a shortcut through the park.

"I've just finished *Highland Fling*," Anna blurts out.

"You what?" I've seen Anna dancing; it's not pretty.

"It's a 'Hearts and Flowers' novel; you obviously haven't read it then. It's about this woman called Savannah who moves with her husband and young son to the Scottish Highlands but her husband is a real jerk and ignores her and stuff so she starts taking long walks every day and stumbles upon this gorgeous ancient castle and starts exploring the gardens where she meets the lord of the castle who's a real hard-head called Duncan Mac-something-or-other and they have this fat argument and she hates him until he sees her swimming naked in the loch—not the same one with the monster I don't think—and they end up falling passionately in love and he gives her the attention she craves and they have this steamy affair until hubby finds out but it's fine because it turns out he's gay anyway."

Anna's not doing the plot many favors. "Let me guess, you've been snooping in Mum's cupboard again then?" I respond.

"So what! This 'Hearts and Flowers' business is quite different and a whole lot more interesting than the birds 'n' bees blabber we get dished out at school."

I don't say anything, but Anna has a point. Sex ed class is all mucus and membranes and as appealing as hair in a plughole. I was rather wondering what all the fuss and excitement was about, but the guys and girls at "Hearts and Flowers" have cleared things up for me. I think I've got it all figured out now, thank you very much.

"We should probably stop sneaking them though; you know Mum's bound to catch us out eventually," I say instead.

"Oh, don't be such a wuss, Ella Mental. She'll only catch us if we're clumsy. I'm sure she's forgotten they're even there. I hope she has. Omigod, I hope the units don't—you know—like read them together or something!" The outrageous thought pulls Anna's features into a drawstring knot.

"Oh, gross, can we change the subject, please?" I reply, and recoil from the nauseating notion of our parents having a sex life. I'm sure they've stopped doing it by now. Surely.

"Since discovering 'Hearts and Flowers' I can't wait to get a boyfriend," Anna sighs. "I need a strong man to sweep me off my feet and make me a woman."

"Anna!" I laugh.

"It's fine for you, you've got Toby," Anna continues, "but it's not that easy when you've got a career to consider, you know." I have a problem with this conversation on so many levels I'm not sure how to even begin to respond to this last statement. As it turns out I don't have to, because Anna is content to waffle on. "You have no idea how lonely it gets. You have Toby who needs and wants you. I have no one."

"Well, you'll be raking in the money soon enough and won't even care," is my valiant attempt to conclude the subject.

"Oh, you don't understand the first thing I'm feeling!" Anna shouts and steps up her pace. Unfortunately this is true, although I'd be more willing to try if she would just leave Toby and me out of it, but I don't say anything and move my legs to keep speed with hers. Fate is keeping excellent time because as we round the bend into the station end of High Street, there it is: the most recent poster of my sister, accessorized by products available from Marks & Spencer. This time she's posing with fresh flowers wrapped in green and gold cellophane and a box of chocolates, which I have to admit makes a more attractive picture than the steaming baguette.

"You see," I exclaim cheerfully, "fame and fortune!"

"Oh, what would you know about it," Anna humps without pausing to even glance at her enlarged image. Something must be up.

"Well, I know that you're the one who wanted to do this modeling business in the first place, so what are you moaning about now?"

"It's not as great as you think it is, Ella. It's not all 'fame and fortune,' as you put it."

"What is it then?" I sigh patiently.

"More people hate it than love it," she replies quietly, slowing down a little. "I'm getting it in the neck from some of the kids at school, the girls especially—calling me names like Naomi Campbell-Soup and Deli Diva."

"They're just jealous cows," I snort angrily. I had no idea she was having a hard time of it.

"It doesn't matter *why* they do it; I still have to live with it. If I carry on modeling, that is..."

"But this is something you're good at, Anna—and you enjoy it so much. Don't let them take it away from you. Who are they in your life anyway?"

"Who are they? They're the girls I have to spend five days out of every seven with, that's who!" she responds, looking fiercely vulnerable.

How can I argue with that? Of course I know

that one day we'll look back on these girls with their pointed sticks and poisonous stones and they won't matter to us one single bit. But I also realize that just because everything will one day be okay does not necessarily make it okay right now. As we grow older we'll forget what people said and we'll forget what they did, but it might take us longer to forget how they made us feel. And right now these girls have made my sister feel stupid and hideous instead of bright and beautiful, and that's probably the worst thing you can do to Anna. She leads with her looks; that's where her confidence begins.

I hear the whoosh of the train pulling into Dunton station and in the midst of Anna's crisis I force myself to focus on the unrelated and badly timed reality that in about five seconds a tide of commuters will wash down the stairs and over us.

"Come on, let's get moving," I order and take Anna's elbow, which is shaking. It's shaking because she's crying. "Let's move to the side at least," I soften, eager to feel the cool safety of a solid-brick wall pressing against our backs before the masses descend. Anna allows me to push her against the corrugated brick of the wall and just in time too. I don't even attempt to say another word until the trampling torrent has subsided, and when it does I notice that Lucas and his blur of rusty curls is bringing up the rear. He's surrounded by three unkempt boy-men with wild eyes. They're as thin and hard as sapling whips and look like they might hurt as much too. I've seen these lads before—or ones just like them anyway. They live in the countryside in large, traveling groups and either make off with or damage almost everything in their path.

They're walking very close to Lucas, almost pinning him in—while he looks deceptively carefree. When they get to just a few meters from where Anna and I are standing the shortest of the boys pushes himself up against Lucas's thinness so that his forehead is at chin-butting height. Lucas doesn't resist and shuffles backward until his shoulder blades are touching the same wall Anna and I are taking refuge against. For a few moments everything is unnaturally calm and quiet. It often is before something violent happens.

It's also just at this moment that I get an expectedly clear view straight through to Lucas. I watch as his spirit retreats to the safety inside him, leaving his eyes empty and his body bowed in anticipation of what's to come. He's boarding up for the storm. Something went wrong, but it's too late now—the wild cats are already coiled up and ready to pounce. The short boy discharges a swift burst of movement, plowing his knee directly into Lucas's groin. When it comes to understanding pain, Mrs. Jankowski's husband and my strange friend suddenly have a lot more in common. Lucas winces but doesn't buckle, which may be his mistake. The goon with dark feathery hair only needs one step to carry his fist to Lucas's forehead. When it's just an inch away he begins grinding his jagged knuckles into Lucas's skull like they're the pestle and his bone is the mortar. Lucas tries to stretch from the sharp fist but Shorty grabs a handful of rust and brutally yanks his head lower. Outraged, Feather Head stops with the grinding and starts pelting Lucas with short, vigorous knuckle punches to the head instead.

I have a horrible suspicion that this is just their warm-up routine and I know I must do something, but what if they're carrying knives? These boys usually do, in which case I suppose I *have* to do something. The street has emptied around us, but the newsagent's door—the same one I enter every month to buy my copy of

CosmoGIRL!—is about ten paces away. And if anyone knows about the in-case-of-emergency-break-glass alarm behind the till counter, it's this *Cosmo* girl!

Forgetting about Anna entirely I rip myself from the wall and soar into the familiar newsagent looking for the familiar face of Mr. Singh. He's hiding behind his familiar mask of calm courtesy and doling out change.

"Mr. Singh!" I yell.

He recognizes me instantly and lets a grin slip through the mask. "Miss *CosmoGIRL!*"

"I can't talk now," I breathlessly begin, "there's an emergency . . . a, uh, huge fire . . . please ring the alarm quickly."

"Whaaa?"

"There's no time, PLEASE!"

Mr. Singh's only son is a decorated policeman with very impressive stories and the old man has been waiting a lifetime for a moment of his own. He quickly grabs the alarm's dangling miniature hammer and shatters the glass. The quiet explodes with a pulsating screech and suddenly everyone is clutching their ears and scrambling for the door, everyone except for Mr. Singh—who has dreamt of keeping control of the chaos and ensuring that everyone makes it out alive. I watch this all with a very large seed of guilt wedged in my conscience but I don't have time to feed or water it and quickly rush outside too.

My plan has worked; the three sleazoids have stepped back from Lucas and are looking around in confusion. Everything is suddenly loud and chaotic, which is less conducive to a beating (or to despair, it seems), and even Anna has recovered her senses and dried out and straightened up again.

"What have you done now, crazy girl?" she shouts over the alarm.

"Come on!" I shout back. We scurry close to Lucas and I gesture toward him. He sees me and stealthily slips from his distracted attackers unnoticed. We pick up the pace and keep on running until the squeal of the alarm is nothing more than a vague background distraction.

"Who were those boys?" I finally gasp, panting for air.

"Oh, them . . ." Lucas puffs, and folds over at the waist like a flip phone. "Just some jerks looking for a ding-dong."

"But why do they want to fight with you?" I pant.

"Maybe they just don't appreciate the gift of music." He laughs like this is nothing new.

Anna raises an eyebrow questioningly but doesn't say anything. Lucas had better be telling me the truth because I just betrayed Mr. Singh—father of a fancy policeman and my favorite magazine man in the world—for him and his supposed gift, I think to myself.

Chapter 20
Letter Bomb

I've been very worried about Lucas and I definitely need to talk to someone about the boys who tried to beat him up, and considering that Toby is my best friend (AND boyfriend of course) and Tom-Tom is sort of the best mate Lucas has, catching the two of them together really is the bonus prize. And Toby just happens to be visiting Tom-Tom, so today must be my lucky day. I ring the chime and wait for the footsteps and the door to Tom's house to swing open.

"Hey, Ellie." It's Toby; he was expecting me.

"Hey, Tobes." I grin and sigh. I could see him one thousand billion times and yet still never ever tire of his bright blue eyes that flicker like sparklers and today seem to have a smidgen of silver in them. He's wearing his Umbro T-shirt that has a picture of a soccer ball and the words *If you ain't a player, wear something else* printed on the front. He looks super-yummy-with-toppings in this shirt.

These days I'm brave enough to initiate a

kiss, and I step forward and set my lips down on his like they're delicate crystal. I don't do the tongue thing though; cool, casual kisses are just as nice sometimes, I believe (this has nothing to do with the Good Sense Guide, mind you). Toby puts his arms around my waist and responds with a cuddle, which makes a cool, casual kiss just about the best thing in the world.

"How are you today?" He smiles. I'm still grinning. To the world you may be one person but to me you are the world, mister! I read that somewhere and it's a catchphrase for my love. "Ella?" Toby repeats.

"Uh . . . yah, I'm brilliant!" I gush. I have two extremes, but no middle ground it seems.

"Here, I want to show you something," he says, ignoring my madness and stepping back from the door.

I trail him inside and find Tom-Tom with his nose to the PC screen. "Hey, Tom, what are you looking at?"

"Hi, Ella," Tom-Tom sighs. "I'm not entirely sure."

He pushes his wheely chair backward and gives me room to take a peak for myself. My heart decelerates; it's a message from Tin Man.

H'Lo Peeps,

This world is full of posers, man. I'm just so tired of it. You all bore me. I need to go find my peace, because I won't find it here in this world. It's like that Don McLean geezer says—

I'm suffering for my sanity,
I'm trying to set you free,
But this world was never meant for one as beautiful as me,
You won't listen,
You're not listening still,
Perhaps you never will.
I knew I'd never make old bones, so what's the point in sticking around.
Good luck, you're all gonna need it.
S'Long,
Tin Man

I read his message over again; this is not good. How serious is he? This Tin Man hopscotch-leaps from vulnerable to hostile and back again. He's up and down and all over the place and it's almost impossible to guess what he's really about.

I doubt even he knows, come to think of it.

"What's your verdict?" Toby asks.

"I've read some of his other postings," I admit. "I don't know what his problem is . . . but it's probably hard to pronounce."

"He does seem a bit off the wall, doesn't he," Toby agrees, nodding.

"We have two issues here," Tom-Tom says efficiently, like he's following on from a discussion that took place before I arrived. "Firstly, this guy sounds like he could be suicidal." Toby and I don't answer but once again nod solemnly in agreement. "Secondly, this is my website, so I'm responsible for reporting this to somebody."

"I've replied to one of his messages before," I suddenly volunteer. This is heavy stuff; I must tell them absolutely everything I know.

"You have? Where . . . when?" Tom-Tom asks, shaking the computer mouse back to life again ready to search for my posting.

The very last thing I want to do is introduce either lads to Lilac Laserin, but what choice do I have? With cheeks the color of chili peppers I slide the mouse from Tom-Tom's grip and scroll up to the message in question. I highlight it but don't say a word and everything is silent while

Toby and Tom-Tom get in the loop and familiarise themselves with my posting.

Toby is the first to remark. "Who is Lilac Laserin?" He smears the name with his lips, like I called myself Belinda Bootylicious or something equally bizarre.

"It's called an alias, and I happen to think Lilac is a lovely name," I sniff haughtily, and hold a mental prayer meeting that he won't decipher the anagram.

"If you're a porn star maybe," he replies.

"And what do you know about porn stars then?" I ask.

"I think we're straying from the topic here," Tom-Tom interrupts. "Ella, or should I say . . . er, Lilac, that was good advice you gave Tin Man. Unfortunately it doesn't sound as if he did approach anybody for help. He sounds more distressed than ever."

"That's true." I nod and shelve Toby's porn-star comment for another time. Dad says women are good at doing that.

"I'm going to contact Childline about this message," Tom-Tom decides. "This is one for the professionals. They can probably trace the e-mail address and find out who Tin Man really is, and hopefully where he lives." Toby and I nod in agreement. "And I guess I should phone rather than e-mail them." We both nod to that too. "I suppose I could get the number off their website." For all our nodding I think Tom-Tom's forgotten we're here.

"Do you want us to hang around?" Toby asks.

"Nah, this is a one-man job—not much you guys can do."

"Right, well, call me with an update when you're done mate," Toby replies, and then adds, "and don't feel bad—if it wasn't your website Tin Man would most certainly have found another one." Nobody reads minds like Toby.

"Thanks, mate." Tom-Tom smiles gratefully.

I feel rather guilty about abandoning Tom-Tom but Toby knows him best, so if we're leaving perhaps it's because Tom-Tom takes his responsibilities very seriously and needs to apply himself without any distractions or interference from us.

"I've got the *MTV Video Music Awards* on tape—do you want to come over to mine and watch it?" Toby asks when we're outside and walking from Tom-Tom's red-brick house.

"Sure." I nod. "Any chance of Daftcow being

there too?" When Melanie's around Toby and I can't even *sit* next to each other without her making singsong taunts and smooching sounds.

"She's visiting the sperm donor," he replies.

Toby still hasn't forgiven his dad for leaving his mum for the non-Mrs. T woman, even though it's been a while since he moved out. He won't even speak to him on the phone yet. I understand his feelings, but there's no sense in him canceling his dad out completely over this. It won't change anything. Toby's never spoken the words, but I know him well enough to recognize that he feels personally betrayed in this too. He and his dad were so close that at times the edges separating them seemed blurry. It's not just the leaving that Toby finds unforgivable, but what took place before and leading up to that day that he's struggling to come to terms with. There were secrets he never even suspected; a side to his hero he'd never been shown or knew existed. And now he's got to relearn his father all over again. Just how long does it take to grieve for the loss of a flawless childhood idol?

Toby's forehead has turned as dark as February, which tells me that it's time to change the subject. "Anna's pretty miserable at the moment," I begin. "It seems that some of the girls at school are giving her a tough time about the M&S posters—calling her 'Deli Diva' and that sort of thing. Girls really are spiteful bullies." Speaking of bullies reminds me of why I came to see Toby in the first place, and I immediately start recounting the events that led up to and including the fire alarm. Toby knows better than to interrupt me when I've got the chatter-bug and only when he's sure that I'm completely empty does he transform my monologue into a conversation.

"You set the alarm off?" he eventually asks.

"Well I didn't, but Mr. Singh did," I reply.

"Ella Mental . . ." he sighs, and shakes his head, but thankfully drops the subject of my guilt. "I had heard that Lucas gets picked on a bit. Mike—our goalie—is his neighbor and has known him for like ever. He says Lucas does sometimes wind people up though."

"Why didn't you tell me?" I ask. Is the art of communication completely lost on these blokes?

"What for, it's none of our business."

Like that's relevant, I want to snort but don't. "He told me he's bipolar," I say instead. I don't really feel bad about blabbing any more, I just can't keep this all to myself. "It's actually called bipolar disorder, which is another name for manic depression. I read up on it and it's really quite serious. He's seeing a psychiatrist and takes medication for it, which is why he can't do certain jobs like work with heavy machinery and stuff. It pretty much explains why one day he's full of the joys of Lucas and then the next day he's got a face like Marilyn Manson."

"Who?"

"The singer with the evil makeup and bleached eye," I sigh. Sharing with Toby is a bit one-dimensional and not quite as elaborate as chatting with the girls.

"I'll check that he's not in any serious trouble, okay?" Toby offers. "But this really isn't our business. Lucas isn't a child, Ella."

"I guess not," I agree halfheartedly. But at least Toby is willing to take some action (which means that he must have learned something from the Jimmy Fake-Tan incident).

"Dating you is a full-time job . . . I should get danger pay," Toby groans, and then stretches his strides.

A full-time job? So is that like a good or a bad

thing then, I wonder as I pump my legs like two well-oiled pistons in order to catch a glimpse of Toby's face. I'm actually really easy to get along with once you learn to see it my way. Honest.

Chapter 21
Sex for Dummies

We've been sitting in Mrs. Turner's classroom for more than ten minutes now, waiting for her to make an appearance and teach us all about the wonderful world of long ago. I'm lousy at remembering dates, but I do like history. Mrs. Turner says that you need to know where you come from to know where you're going, which makes sense. It's the present she seems to have a problem with. You'd think she could at least show up on time; you've got to be crazy to leave this lot alone for too long.

Ivor McDougal, aka "Big Mac" (he's small but fearless, as if he were really ten stories high) is sitting across from me and biting off bits of his eraser and spitting the pieces at Priscilla Pearson's back. Everyone calls her "Miss Priss," which I have to admit she does sort of ask for—most of the time she acts fifteen going on fifty. I'm only watching Big Mac and Miss Priss because I have nothing else to do. Every time he launches a gobby bit of rubber at her she spins around, pushes her glasses up to her forehead, puckers her lips, and glares at him, while he just sits there grinning at her until she finally turns around again, and then he spits again and she spins and puckers again. They've been going on like this forever and I'm gagging to tell her to simply ignore him (can't she see that she's turned a simple league game into a Cup Final?), but I know better than to attract Big Mac's attention. This isn't school, it's hell with fluorescent lighting.

Suddenly a voice booms from above. For a moment I think it's the divine intervention I've been praying for, but then I realize that it's actually Mr Povey, our headmaster, speaking over the intercom.

"Would all Year 10 and 11 pupils please file quietly down to the main hall where you will be shown a movie that will last until first break."

The room ripples with a low grumble (I don't participate; right now a slap in the mouth with a halibut is better than watching Big Mac and Priss). Mr Povey also remains silent; he's taking a moment to dip into the mind of a teenager. They can't roll-call the movie so chances are most of the kids will skive off and either set fire to or smoke whatever they can lay their hands on.

"It's a movie about sex," he adds quickly. Time stops. Nobody moves, not even to breathe. Sex? "Yes that's right, I said sex. Now would you all please get moving."

The floor growls with the onslaught of scraping chairs. I glance around the classroom; Big Mac is long gone but Priscilla is slowly packing up the pens, pencils, and books she had neatly laid out on her desk in readiness for our trip down memory lane. The glistening bits of eraser still stuck in her hair look almost pretty, like small, shiny, freshwater pearls. Still, I know I wouldn't want them in my hair.

"You probably want to shake your hair out, Priscilla," I say as I walk past her desk en route to the door. She doesn't reply but just glares at me instead, like I was the one who spat them there. Sometimes I just don't know why I bother.

The corridor is all bobbing heads and I arc my eye across the swells, searching for my friends. Sex movie or no sex movie, I don't want to sit there on my own. I'll even settle for sexed-up Anna at this point, although she's probably in the main hall already, sitting front and center next to Big Mac. It takes a few moments but I finally spy a face I recognize for all the right reasons; it's Toby and he's heading toward me. At least we can sit next to . . .

Like a flashing neon sign that spells out the words *VERY BAD IDEA*, the mortifying vision of Toby and me sitting side by side watching a movie about sex suddenly projects before me, making the nerves in my right eyelid twitch and both armpits perspire (I'm usually blessed with unnaturally dry armpits, so this has got to be bad). I flick my eyes this way and that; there's nowhere to run or hide and if I drop to floor I'll probably get trampled to death.

"Hey, Ellie, what's going on?" my love greets me.

"Uh, sex movie?" I offer with just a hint of high-pitched panic in my voice.

"No, I mean with the teachers. Mr. Sangster never showed up."

Ah, right. "Neither did Mrs. Turner. Maybe they had to have an emergency crisis teacher meeting convention. Or something or uh . . . other?" I blither.

"Yeah, maybe. Come on, let's get moving."

Using my elbow as a rudder Toby steers us toward the current of eager teenagers and we allow ourselves be swept along to the main hall where we manage to maneuver into two of the few remaining seats. The first and only thing I notice before the lights fade away is the projection screen dangling from the ceiling like a bright white banner still waiting for a reason. Nothing happens for a few seconds, and then all of a sudden a spectrum of colorful light splashes onto the screen, finally giving it purpose. It's pretty, but illegible—until somebody finds the focus button. Now the screen says:

The Department of Health
Getting Educated About Sex

Toby tenses up instantly; he's just figured it out. I keep glowing-face front and sense him sliding down deeper into his molded plastic chair, probably hoping to disappear into it completely. Too late now, buddy, I squirm. Five seconds would have done it—that's all I needed to run for it. What I'd give to be hanging out with the faggers and the pyromaniacs now! But we're trapped, doomed to sit here and pretend that we're mature young adults capable of watching our dangly bits being paraded about on a giant-size screen. Giant dangly bits...if giants even have dangly bits. I think I may be out of my mind, in which case please leave a message.

The titles fade to reveal two cartoon figures—a boy in square pants and a girl dressed in a pretty, purple triangle. At least they're wearing clothing, that's something. A female voice-over begins narrating the visuals: "Not only do boys and girls look different on the outside, but they look different on the inside too." The speakers quiver with the sound of bells tinkling—like a magic wand that's being waved, and with the bells go the clothes. All of them! The square pants and the purple triangle suddenly vanish into the ether, leaving us faced with what I can only describe as X-rated animation. Talk about comic strip!

As an optimist I suppose the good news is that we're not into close-ups and for the moment—if I flatten my eyes into slits and think pure thoughts, I can just about think of the naked cartoon bits in terms of a fruit machine. A banana, a couple of grapes, a peach or two with a strawberry thrown in for good measure, it's not the jackpot but it'll do.

Had I been watching this sex movie with

anybody other than Toby I probably wouldn't give a hoot. In fact, I'd probably find it a real hoot! But sitting beside my childhood soul mate, current boyfriend, and future husband, who has just recently admitted to noticing my breasticles changes things a little. Watching this movie together and learning about his bits while he learns about mine is a little too close for comfort. I'll have that slap in the mouth with a halibut now, thanks very much.

The voice and the pictures continue, oblivious to my pain as I watch and listen without stirring or breathing. There's a small chance Toby will forget I'm there. The irritating voice-over woman with the hot-potato accent is warbling on as casually as if she were an air stewardess pointing out the location of the emergency exits and inflatable life jackets. And there it is! Suddenly we're into close-ups. Now it's all bright colors and moving diagrams with arrows and labels for those who still aren't sure what goes where (who knew that "sperm" is really short for *spermatozoon*?). This movie could put a girl off for life.

Chapter 22
He Ain't Heavy

It's Saturday morning and Mum and I are driving home in Bluebell after dropping Anna off at Aunt Chloe's office. Anna was supposed to return home with us; she was apparently only going there to break the news that she no longer wanted to be the face of Marks & Spencer, but when we got there Aunt Chloe was showing a boy called Julio around. Julio, it seems, is now the male face of M&S and the new Christmas advertising campaign is going to feature a girl and a boy striding along with tinsel and turkeys.

Anna set eyes on Julio and dribbled all over Aunt Chloe's handmade Italian leather pumps. And if I hadn't seen it for myself I'd never have believed it in a million years: Julio is *the image* of Tucker from *Flames of Passion*! A little younger, sure, but he even has the same wavy, blond hair and small, arched, brown nose. We'd have needed a crowbar to get Anna to leave that boy's side.

"Does Julio remind you of anyone?" Mum suddenly asks, gripping the steering wheel tightly.

Her eyes are on the road but they're narrowed, as if she's trying to peer all the way down memory lane and focus on the various faces along the way. Tucker must have made an impression on her too!

I know that if I give in to the hysterical giggle pushing at my lips I'll lose it completely. Not only that, but my mother will get very suspicious and start tightening the screws to get me to talk—just what I don't need. So I smother my smile with my hand, breathe deep, and gaze out the window at the passing scenery instead. The air streaming in through Bluebell's decayed air vent is pleasantly cool without being chilling, and I position myself so that most of it lands on my neck. In winter I practically have to wrap up like an Eskimo and lie horizontal to escape its arctic flow, but today I'm in short sleeves and looking out at gorgeous blue skies. Mum doesn't seem bothered that I haven't replied to her question and we continue the drive home in easy silence. I've got some Toby-dreaming to catch up on.

The grind of Bluebell's ancient engine as Mum gears down ends my quiet reverie. We're still blocks from home. "We haven't got to stop for something, have we?" I groan. I've got things to do and a boyfriend to see.

"I'm slowing down because a policeman is telling me to!" Mum snaps. I turn face front and see her point. A policeman in a luminous yellow waistcoat is standing in the road and urging us to pass slowly. The park behind him—the same one Anna and I have spent a lifetime cutting across—is a vision of swirling lights, brightly striped police tape, and busy uniforms all melting into one another and it takes a few moments for the image to settle in my head.

"What is going on?" I gasp.

"I don't know," Mum mumbles as she guides Bluebell along.

As the car crawls forward my view is blocked by a big white van with the words *Emergency Services* printed on its side, so I set my sights on the policeman in the yellow waistcoat instead. As we pass within a few feet of him it feels like time has slowed right down and I observe through the passenger window his bent elbow and cupped hand gesturing us on. His movements seem as slow and smooth as if they were cutting through water. I'm staring so hard I somehow manage to catch and drag his gaze down toward me. His mouth and jaw are official and closed to the public, but his eyes are glazed and confused. Whatever has taken place here today—

whatever code they've been called out on—for this policeman it's a first-time event, and he's still trying to make sense of it all.

We slide past and the policeman finally returns his gaze to the line of cars behind us, and as he does so time suddenly finds its usual pace again. Nothing is slow and thick anymore, and Mum is muttering to herself.

"Oh my, I hope there wasn't a motorbike accident . . . the kids of today . . . so reckless." She recently watched a documentary on the teenage biker gangs of Tokyo, and I think she sees the village of Dunton going the same way. But I don't say anything and we drive the rest of the way in thoughtful silence.

We reach home to find Dad stoking a barbecue on the front lawn. He's got his shirt off so that the entire world and any peeping-Tom aliens can see his eagle tattoo, and I'm willing to bet that he'll offer to show me how the wings expand when he flexes the flabby bits he refers to as his muscles (in 1970 maybe). As if barbecuing on the front lawn isn't mortifying enough!

"Hey, girls, look what I'm doing here!" he yells out to us.

Uh, embarrassing the entire Watson family—

past, present, and future, perhaps? "Hi, Dad," I sigh dismally. Experience has taught me to keep my cheeky comments in my head; I only end up the loser if I let them out.

"Do you want to see an eagle soar?" he grins at me.

"Ah, no." I have to go stick a pencil in my eye. "But thanks anyway."

I trudge indoors and briefly catch a glimpse of Dad striking an Incredible Hulk pose on the front lawn while Mum coos over the poor worn-out eagle for the zillionth time. "Hearts and Flowers" publish stories especially for women just like my mother, I reflect. I'm about to head upstairs when I remember that it's my week to mow the patch of green that is our back garden, which is probably why Dad is barbecuing on the front lawn. He may forget many things—like putting petrol in the car and what time we eat dinner, but he *never* forgets a chore. So shoving my mobile in my back pocket and tying my hair in a ponytail, I trundle out to the shed. It's not that I'm particularly diligent; I just hate being told what to do.

By the time the lawn is neat and trimmed I'm hot and bothered and I decide to shower and change and check PPT's most recent postings before I call Toby. There's nothing from Tin Man, not a peep. Perhaps Childline made contact with him after all. I'm just about to dial Toby's number when the phone suddenly starts vibrating and ringing in my hand, practically scaring the freshly laundered pants off me.

"Hello?" I gulp.

"Hey, Ellie, it's Toby." We have a psychic love connection.

"Hey, Tobes." I grin.

"What are you doing?"

"Not much, you?"

"Not much."

"Cool."

"Yah. Cool."

Pause.

"So do you remember that goalie named Mike I told you about, the one who lives next door to Lucas?" he asks.

"Uh huh."

"Well, he just rang me, says the cops are over at Lucas's house."

"That's not good!" I gasp. Don't tell me there's been more fighting.

"And no, there's zip we can do about it or him or anything," Toby quickly adds.

Until this year policemen were colorful characters on telly—nothing more, and yet these days they seem to be regular visitors with a gold membership to my life. If it's not the *poopy* patrol then it's the Friendly Interrogators Margie and Eileen. And today is a shining example: they're all around me. I grow older and this planet gets crazier. Coincidence? I'm starting to think not.

"But shouldn't we . . . uh, do *something*?" It's all I have right now.

"Well, how about you come over and we watch a DVD?"

"Yes, you're right," I declare, sitting upright. "I'll come around and we can phone your goalie and find out more."

"It sounds like English but I can't understand a word you're saying, Ella Mental," Toby responds dryly. "Now get your rear into gear and I'll get the DVD warmed up."

I hang up and find my mobile. All I want to do is get over to Toby's as quickly as possible but I have to bypass my father, his eagle, and the burgers he's cremating on the barbecue first.

"Flap flap," Dad says, grinning and winking knowingly at the eagle that might easily be mistaken for a dodo bird. I must be adopted, surely.

"No thanks, Dad," I say, and hurry down the garden path. Perhaps the cops need to pay a visit to our house too; a man my father's age should not be going around topless.

By the time I reach Toby's I'm breathless but full up with ideas about how we can help Lucas. I'm just about to reach for the front door handle when the door swings open forcefully to reveal Pearl, who has the other side of the handle in her grip.

"Pearl?" I stutter.

"You'd better come in, Ella," she says dramatically.

I couldn't agree more, I think to myself as I step inside. Hasn't she got enough boys to hang about with!

Toby suddenly appears in the hallway. "Hey, Ellie." His skin has an unusual floury tinge to it, his lips are stretched tight, and his eyes seem glassy and too big for his face, and for a short flash of an instant he reminds me of a ventriloquist-dummy version of his normal self. Something is very wrong.

"What's the matter?" I ask.

"Here, why don't you sit down," he suggests, ushering me into the living room like some weirdo butler.

I know my way to the living room, I'm tempted to shout, but manage to restrain my panic. I'm already thinking the worst, which is the worst thing about not knowing. Pearl follows us but nobody says anything.

"What?" I demand once again.

"Something has happened to Lucas," Pearl begins. She's putting on a very grown-up act but I can see her brightly painted fingertips trembling at her side. The doorbell rings and Toby bolts out of his chair like an Olympic athlete to answer it. Neither Pearl nor I move; we just sit there staring manically at one another. She attempts a small, sad smile, which I think is meant to be reassuring but just makes me want to throttle her. Suddenly Toby reappears with Tom-Tom and Frannie in tow. I make contact with Frannie's eyes; they're red and bewildered. I'm not sure, but it looks like Tom-Tom's been crying too.

"What is going on?" I shout loudly, bouncing my eyes from one friend to the next like a pinball on a winning streak.

"Lucas is dead," Pearl says, and then starts crying.

"No, he's not!" I scoff. I know about his bipolar disorder, remember? He probably just had a fit or something. Do bipolar people have fits? I'm sure they do. And it's not like doctors know everything about every single disease in the whole entire world anyway, do they? So Lucas might be the first bipolar to have a fit, but like my gran says, there's got to be a first time for everything.

"He is dead, Ella," Toby says quietly.

"My mum's been working at the hospital," Pearl continues, except her sobs are loud and coming from so deep inside her that I can hardly prise one word from the next. "She's nursing at Emergency Services." Pearl pauses to wipe her soggy eyes on her pale, cotton sleeve and leaves a long black mascara trail across her forearm. That's definitely going to stain. And yeah, so what? I heard the words "Emergency Services," but it's easier to think about other things right now. Like how Pearl always has to exaggerate and make a production out of everything. It's one Pearlodrama after the next!

"And Mum wanted to be the one to tell me that . . . that they found Lucas's body hanging from a tree in the park. He was already dead when they got there. Mum met Lucas the day we all went to the funfair, so she knew we were friends. She didn't want anyone else to be the one to tell me . . ."

Well, that's just stupid! What's that got to do with having a fit anyway? It just doesn't make any sense. Fran's lower lip has disappeared into her mouth and her face is dimpled and quivering. She suddenly sucks in a great mouthful of air and then starts shaking with quiet mournful sobs. Tom-Tom puts his arms around her and also starts crying. He isn't making any noise but his shoulders are bent and heaving so I can tell.

I remain unmoving and simply watch my friends—usually so bright with white light, now swathed in the dark shadows of grief and sadness—like I'm the cold face of the clock sitting on the mantlepiece and this has nothing whatsoever to do with me. Of course I feel pity for their pain—nobody likes a broken heart, and there's Lucas to consider in this too, but we only saw him a few days ago, didn't we? In fact the last time I saw him was when we made our narrow escape from those dirtbags. I can still recall the shrill shriek of Mr. Singh's alarm in my ears and Lucas, Anna, and me bent over and out of breath after spending it all on running. Lucas's usually pale cheeks were like red mottled stains and his eyes were twinkling with the threat of a chase and the glorious victory of escape. I remember that day, and his strong vibrant presence. So how can he *possibly* be dead and hanging from a tree? And that's when I feel the hard, painful punch to my stomach.

"But wha . . . *WHY?*" I cry out with the last bit of air I have left in me. I feel like I've been dropped in the middle of a black, raging ocean and I've sunk all the way to the bottom without a mask or an oxygen tank for company. I can't see out of my eyes anymore—everything is wet and blurry; it's icy cold and my chest feels as though it might implode from the enormous crushing weight of the pressure pushing down on me. I can't stay upright; I know I'm going to topple over and be swept away.

Suddenly I'm in Toby's arms and I can breathe again. We press our bodies together for warmth and he starts rocking me, all the while cooing and stroking my hair like I'm a delicate mermaid that's been washed up on the beach. I allow myself to be cuddled for a bit, and then struggle and slip from his embrace.

"Why was he hanging from a tree?" I demand through my tears.

"He committed suicide, Ellie," Toby says in a

broken voice. I blink hard to clear my eyes; my lovely's face is puffy and wet.

"But why, Toby?" I ask this like he knows the answer to every question ever made.

"We don't know."

"Well, what does your mum say, Pearl?" I ask.

"Only what I told you," she replies, tearing at the sodden tissue in her hand.

"Did he leave a note?"

"We don't know," Toby repeats.

"Well, we're his friends," I shout loudly, "we have a right to know." I think we may be the only friends he had too. He was the loneliest person I ever met. Is that why he wanted to die? Weren't we enough for him? That would be so bad. We should have tried harder.

Frannie steps forward. "Come, let's sit in a circle on the floor," she says softly, "and hold hands and say a prayer for Lucas."

We do as we're told and form a bond with our hands. It really doesn't matter that my friends and I were born into different faiths or into none at all. What matters is that we connect our hearts with our minds and ask that which is greater than ourselves to guide Lucas's soul to a place of peace, love, and light. I know there's such a place—I feel it inside me sometimes, when I'm light-headed with joy or contentment—and I close my eyes and try to find that place again. After a while I can see Lucas standing before me and I imagine my prayers covering him, insulating him in their warmth and goodness. I don't seem to understand anything anymore, but perhaps I'm not ready. Maybe that time will come.

Chapter 23
Ghost Writer

It's almost eleven o'clock in the morning but I still don't feel like getting out of bed. I can't really think of a reason to. We all stayed at Toby's until quite late last night, just talking and hanging out. When I phoned Mum and told her about Lucas she was very sympathetic and even offered to come and fetch me any time I wanted. Just then my bedroom door shudders with a knock.

"Ella?" That's Mum's voice.

"Yes?" I'd really just like to be left alone to sleep.

The door opens and Mum enters, carrying a tabloid newspaper in her grip. "You're going to see this eventually," she begins, "so you might as well see it here and now." She hands me the newspaper and sits down gently on the edge of my bed. I soak up the front page emblazoned with the headline: LOCAL BOY HANGS HIMSELF.

Positioned below right of the headline is a photo of Lucas in his school uniform looking pokerfaced in front of floating, blue studio clouds.

The journalist must have somehow got this from Dunton Secondary.

I prop myself up higher in bed and hold the inky paper close to my nose. Mum switches on my bedside lamp but thankfully skips the you're-going-to-damage-your-eyes dialogue. I skim through the printed copy; apart from the standard stuff (he lived with his parents; had a much older brother; attended Dunton Secondary but then worked odd jobs; loved playing the guitar) the article doesn't give very much information. It doesn't reveal his bipolar disorder, although it does mention two other things that will remain seared on my brain forever: Lucas's seventeenth birthday was just a few days away, and no suicide note was found at the scene or at his home or anywhere. I feel a small tear trickling down the inside of my nose, making it itch. I wipe it away roughly and toss the paper aside.

"I'm sorry Ella," Mum says.

"Yeah, me too," I reply sadly. "I just wish he'd come to one of us for help."

"Can I get you anything?" she asks.

"No, thanks, I just want to sleep."

"Okay, then," she responds, rubbing her hand over mine and switching off the lamp. My mother and I don't usually touch, but it doesn't feel weird. In fact I sort of like it. "I'm off to do some grocery shopping. I'll be back soon." I don't reply and sink down deeper into my duvet. The door clicks shut and I close my eyes and wait patiently for sleep. It's bobbing about on the horizon—almost within touching distance, when my door knocks again. I just want to sleep!

"Ella?" It's Anna this time.

"YES!"

The door clicks open again and Anna stands silhouetted in its frame. "Something came for you this morning," she says.

"What is it?" I growl.

"I don't know. Post."

I never get snail mail; it must be one of the stupid junk mail thingies Mum usually gets. Why Anna feels I need it right this very minute I don't know, but I suppose she's just trying to be helpful.

"Can't you just leave it somewhere and I'll read it later?"

"Sure," she says amicably, "I'll leave it on your bedside table."

She delivers it as promised and slinks out of my room again. If only it were always that easy. I shove my head underneath the covers and scan the horizon for the sleep that was beckoning just a short while ago. I don't see anything, but I hang about in the darkness for a while, hoping it'll make a return trip. Nothing. I suppose I should have a bath; it was the last thing on my mind last night. I snake a hand out of the covers and switch on the lamp once again. Next step: my legs. The rest of my body follows obediently and I sit upright on the same edge of mattress Mum recently vacated and root out my slippers with my toes. My dressing gown is draped over the back of a chair. I'll have to stand up for that one. I slump my chin back down to my chest and decide to think about it for a while first and gather up some energy.

There's the post Anna delivered; one square white envelope with my name and address written in blue ballpoint on the front. I lift it from the bedside table and give it a second glance. It's missing a surname and a postcode. This must have been posted in Dunton. It seems a bit lackadaisical for junk mail or anything official. I flip the envelope over on its belly and start picking at the triangle tip of its mouth. It hasn't been stuck down very well and I've got it open and gutted in no time at all. All that's inside is a single sheet of lined paper. My name isn't mentioned anywhere, but it doesn't take a rocket scientist to recognize that these are the lyrics to a song I don't think I've ever heard before.

COMING IN FROM THE COLD

(Acoustic Version)

They call me the Tin Man, still looking for a heart

It's always been this way, right from the start

There's nothing inside me, it's empty and gray

So what's the point in living, for even one more day?

Consumed by the raging vacuum inside my soul

What would I give? I'd give my life to feel whole

Chorus:

There's a terrible storm coming, you'd better beware

Skies are crashing, there's danger everywhere

Thunder, lightning, rain, and flood

How can this be the start of anything good?

There's a terrible storm coming, you'd better beware

That's how it started, so came my despair

With the yellow brick road stretched up like gold

And all the sadness and sorrow, who'd want to grow old?

My only company: loneliness and music

If this was your life, I doubt you would choose it

The path is before me, my destiny is clear

I can go toward the light and let go of the fear

(Repeat Chorus)

This won't be the end, I've only just begun

I'm finally free, speeding toward the sun

The years of emptiness will all be gone

It's taken a while but I'll be where I belong

It's a long ride home, but I'll have a room with a view

From the darkness to the light, where it's shiny and new

Lyrics and musical arrangement: Tin Man

I think I'm going to be sick. How can this be from Tin Man? We've never even met; *I don't even know who he is!* He may have corresponded with Lilac Laserin, but there's *no way* he could have worked out the anagram. Or could he? And why is he sending me this song in the first place? This is creepy, has he been spying on me? I feel dizzy with questions. My heart is thrashing about in my chest and making it difficult to think. Perhaps I'm just being silly; I've *got* to think. I read the song words over once again, sucking up their flavor and trying to decipher their meaning.

Okay, so I've got the whole *Wizard of Oz* connection—it's one of Mum's favorite movies. But why is he looking for a heart? I think back to his postings on PPT, remembering that he said he felt numb and empty inside. "The skies are crashing . . ." But what can that mean?

And then I understand. My bedroom closes in swiftly around me; casing me in so tightly all I can see are walls—a white cell for crazy people. The suffocating silence crackles and sizzles in my ear like electric snow from a television that can't find a signal, and because I've forgotten to breathe my fingertips and lips have started tingling.

"Lucas is Tin Man," I whisper, finally gasping for air. "He's mailed me his suicide note." I think back to the day we walked home from the library together and how he opened up about his bipolar disorder to me. For some reason he felt he could confide in me, that I would understand him.

"Thunder, lightning, rain, and flood, how can this be the start of anything good?" I murmur. He also told me he was born during one of the worst storms in British history.

I don't have the strength to hold the letter up any longer and let my hands fall weakly to my lap. I stare straight ahead, unmoving and not focusing on anything in particular. Was his emptiness an effect of his bipolar disorder? I try to recall what I'd researched on the subject: something about a brain disorder causing manic depression. When I'm depressed nothing interests me or brings me pleasure, although this feeling never lasts. But what if I magnified this a million times over and felt that way all the time? Only a psychiatrist could say for sure, but it's not unlikely.

I don't realize I'm crying until I glance down and notice that I've leaked all over the letter. But it doesn't belong to me; it should be with Lucas's family! I jump up and grab tissues from the box nearby and start blotting frantically at the dampness. Luckily the pen hasn't run; it'll dry in time. Now what? I'm already exhausted by Lucas's expectations of me.

* * *

I consulted with Toby and Mum and both agreed that the letter should go to the police. We toyed with taking it to Lucas's parents but considering that we're complete strangers and they're submerged deep in their shock and grief, we'd probably have freaked them out. And of course there's a chance we might be wrong about Tin Man, although I know with a primal instinct I can't explain that we're not. Those were absolutely Lucas's final words to the world. Why he chose to send the song to me is something I'll always wonder about. Perhaps the episode outside Mr. Singh's was the greatest act of kindness he'd ever been shown. Who knows—probably nobody. But it was my ball and I ran with it.

The police listened carefully, took pages of spidery notes, and asked the same questions over and over like we were morons out on a jaunt. But I think they believed us in the end. I had to call Tom-Tom about the Childline connection, although he said he didn't know very much and they'd have to contact the organization directly for further information. I also told them about Lucas's bipolar disorder, although they didn't seem surprised—his parents must have told them about this already.

Mum, Toby, and I had already been at the police station for an hour and a half before we finally ran out of things to say. So I stared down at my trainers drumming on the linoleum floor of the room with the desk, chairs, and large mirror and fidgeted with the white quarter-moons of my fingernails while everyone stared at one another expectantly. The police were being thorough; they wanted to be sure so that they wouldn't have to call us back again, which is why I decided to fill the silence with the story about the boys who tried to beat Lucas up outside Mr. Singh's shop. After all, why shouldn't they know what a hard time Lucas had?

"We don't suspect foul play," the oldest policeman with bags like a basset hound barked at me. I looked him in the eye and contemplated suggesting that when dealing with the general public (after all, no crooks in this room!) he take a few tips from the Friendly Interrogators Margie and Eileen, but then I thought better of it. I just wanted to get home.

Chapter 24
Plain Good Sense

Mr. Povey is not usually a man of many words, but today he held a special assembly in Lucas's honor and talked about him as if he were his own son. Death is poignant, no matter how you meet it, but I think we've all been touched by the hopelessness Lucas must have felt before he took his own life. Maybe we all feel responsible in some small way too.

Today would also have been Lucas's birthday, so Fran, Pearl, Tom-Tom, Toby, and I are meeting after school to lay flowers and cards at the tree in the park. I have a card already written in my school bag, and I have money in my pocket to buy flowers on the way. The flowers will be from Toby too. I've got it all worked out. I'm trying to focus on this day and the schoolwork that's expected of me, but my eyeballs won't focus. They keep glazing over and turning in to spy on what's going on in my head instead. When the bell finally rings I almost miss it, but not quite. That's because I've got it all worked out.

We meet outside the school gates (even Pearl is punctual) and start walking in the direction of High Street. There's only one florist in Dunton, but it's not much of a detour from the park. I've decided that I'm going to buy wildflowers, like maybe daisies or lavender; to me Lucas was anything but conventional. The florist's assistant is very helpful and dresses the white daisies in plumes of wild grasses she keeps in a bucket on the stone floor. Pearl buys three radiant sunflowers and has them wrapped in a red-wine bow the color of Lucas's hair, and Fran and Tom-Tom go half-and-half on a beautiful English rose bush they're going to plant at the base of the tree. I wish I'd thought of that; it's ingenious.

Standing beside the front door of the grocers a few shops down from the florist is an upright Plexiglas stand with flaps that open to cubicles housing various newspapers. I don't pay it much attention, but Toby stops walking and lifts one of them open. "Hey guys, take a look here," he says, still staring down.

We all crowd warily around him, careful not to crush our precious flowers. The headline reads:

LOCAL SUICIDE: MORE FACTS COME TO LIGHT

They've used a different photo of Lucas

this time. He's dressed in jeans and a sweater and looks relaxed and happy—even with his broken smile. Toby starts reading out loud.

"'The police are in possession of a suicide note, although any further details regarding its discovery or contents have not yet been released. This confirms the verdict of suicide.

"'New medical information has come to light confirming that Lucas Webster suffered from bipolar disorder, also commonly referred to as manic depression.'" Toby's eyes continue running along the page but his mouth has lost interest. He finally looks up at me and then turns to Pearl, Tom, and Fran.

Pearl has started crying again. "I didn't even know his surname was Webster," she sobs, and starts scratching in her bag for a tissue.

"Do you remember that day at the funfair," Frannie suddenly asks, "the day we met Gypsy Grandma?"

Nobody says anything but we all nod.

"Remember how Lucas asked Gypsy Grandma if he'd ever be famous?" More nods. "And she replied that people near and far would be talking and writing about him for a long time to come." We've all got that faraway look in our eyes, like our minds have left us and are no longer on High Street but back at the funfair with Gypsy Grandma instead.

"And she was right," Tom-Tom whispers, coming back to the present.

Three and a half weeks have passed but instead of time healing, I seem to miss Lucas even more. That's the thing about mortality, I suppose. First there's the heartbreak of death to deal with and then, as the days roll by, you've got to get used to simply not having that person around any more. One day here and the next day gone. I've never lost anyone I cared about before and it's forced me to do some growing up. We entertain ourselves with stories that have happy endings. We even rely on these happy endings. But in real life we don't have that guarantee. In real life you have to strategize, stay focused, and work for your happy ending. You can't cross your fingers and hope for the best. It doesn't *just happen*.

Anna and Julio are on a location shoot today, modeling hats or pots or something, I'm not sure. I wasn't really paying attention. They're also snogging (not while they model but in between). This doesn't mean they're dating though—frantic high-flyers like them just don't have time for romance. No, Anna and Julio (that's a soft "J" mind you, more like a "Sh") just snog every chance they get. Hats, pots, snogs . . . I'm just glad I have the PC to myself for a while. I believe my Elemental Good Sense Guide is as close to ready as it'll ever be and the time has come for me to send it to the editor of *CosmoGIRL!*. Now all I've got to do is write a cover letter selling the whole idea (not that I think it needs selling, but that's just what you do in the professional world of publishing and such).

I was going to begin the letter by telling the editor a bit about myself (my age, hopes, dreams, inner fears, loves, hates, worries, whims—basic stuff), but on second thought I'm probably better off keeping an air of mystery about myself. And I'm worried that if I mention I'm not quite sixteen people will just presume I'm too young to know much about life or having good sense. I battle against these prejudices every day. If only they knew what my friends and I have been through, and how we've emerged weary but magnificent at the other end! Yes, change is inevitable (except from a vending machine); there's not much we can do about that. The trick is to open your arms to it but keep a firm grip on your values.

Tom-Tom put so much thought and effort into Pinboard Psychology for Teens it would have been a tragedy for him to shut the site down after Lucas's death, and for a while I really thought this was going to happen. He had a big scare. But in true Tom-Tom style he has channeled his fears into something positive, and not only is PPT still up and running stronger than ever, but he's now doing volunteer work at Childline. He's decided he wants to become a counselor and then study to be a psychiatrist one day. I try not to go around sprouting too much Good Sense logic but I told Tom that in life the things we most want to forget about tend to be the things we most need to talk about, and I knew he would agree. Tom's also taken it upon himself to turn Gypsy Grandma's prediction into something positive and dedicated PPT to Lucas's memory. He's even included the color photo of Lucas smiling on the opening page. It's not rock 'n' roll, but Lucas would have liked that.

Fran and Tom-Tom have grown really close over the past few weeks and she's talking about joining him at Childline—"even if it's just to make the tea." She's also taken to wearing a thin leather bracelet around her wrist, engraved with the words *Don't let yesterday use up too much of today*. When I asked her about it she said she'd bought it at a car trunk sale and that it was an ancient Cherokee Indian proverb, and exactly how she was going to live the rest of her life. Frannie destroyed her demons, shot them right out of the sky! She blows me away sometimes too. So how could I not include the proverb in the Good Sense Guide? I've credited the Cherokee Indians, of course.

Pearlodrama set fire to her hair last week by smoking a cigarette and using her curling tongs at the same time. She then used her pint-glass of cranberry juice to douse the flames, which stained her singed pale hair a not-so-subtle shade of pink. She was really fed up to begin with but then figured she looked punk, and so has now embraced the look fully by wearing black nail polish and enough eyeliner to rewrite the graffiti on the school walls. Another wash and the pink will have gone, but she's got a bottle of green hair dye ready. She says she's going to protest against the destruction of the rainforest. I tried to explain to her that punk is about being a nonconformist, which is not the same as being a conservationist, but as usual Pearl was having none of it so in the end I just gave up. It's the stirring of a conscience I suppose, and she's very entertaining—you might as well love her.

Of course Toby is still the one for me; I haven't changed my mind about that one bit. In fact, I love him more than ever. And he doesn't seem to have changed his mind either, which is exceptionally good news. We have something not very many couples get right: we're best friends first. The fact that one of us is a girl and the other is a boy is secondary; we're two people who genuinely like each other and enjoy one another's company. That takes awesome precedence over any lusty shenanigans, which is precisely how it should be, I reckon.

The computer screen in front of me is still a blinking white square; I'm doing too much thinking and not enough writing. So I begin by typing my address and all the other stuff that goes at the top of a letter. Right, that was the easy bit. I suppose I really shouldn't intellectualize this too much; I should just write from the heart (although that comes with its own set of risks). Oh, the only way to start is to start!

Dear editor of *CosmoGIRL!*,

My name is Ella Watson and I'm a teenager. I might also be a writer one day (although not even clairvoyants really know what the future holds) so I've been keeping a diary of basic observations about life and the world around me, which I've called the Elemental Good Sense Guide. This might be really useful to your readers who are also just trying to figure it all out.

If you think I'm too young to know very much I would like to politely point out that I am in fact living the teenage experience. And you know what they say: you can learn just about anything, but you can only earn experience (which is sort of like Good Sense Guide logic but not, because I haven't included it). I like to think of myself as the eye of the storm looking out. My friends and I have been through so much already, and this is just the beginning. Every day we make all kinds of choices and decisions. Some are important, others not. But you can't just exist on autopilot and hope for the best because everything has a consequence. That's real life.

Please don't think I think I know everything, because I DEFINITELY DO NOT (although my experience of love, life, and the law is fairly exhausting). Actually, one of the biggest things I've learned is that I still have a lot to learn. But when I don't know the answer I usually try and decide things with an open heart, which sometimes helps. You'll find the rest of the things I've learned attached to this letter. I hope you'll find the Good Sense Guide useful (and maybe print it?). It would be nice if it helped somebody somewhere.

Yours sincerely always and thanks,

Love,
Ella x

P.S. I really liked your last issue, especially the story about losing your virginity. I mean, what's the rush! I'm in a very steady relationship and fairly well-read, so I know there's so much more to love.

The Good Sense Guide

1. Sometimes we believe what we want to believe, because it's easier and less painful in the long run. It can be a dangerous trap.
2. In this life you've got to take what you can get and run with it, because that may be just about all you're getting.
3. A problem doesn't always have to be a biggie to count; what makes a problem important is the fact that it's yours.
4. Don't worry about things until they happen—especially if you have no control over them in the first place.
5. Never trust anyone who is overly nice. They're either insincere fakes or they want something from you.
6. Treat others as you would like them to treat you.
7. Never let the fear of failure be an excuse for not trying. Failure is not a terrible thing, it's part of what makes us human. What would be much worse is if a fear of failure stopped you from trying at all. Just do your best.

8. Everything new seems scary to begin with—especially bad news. Give yourself time to adjust.
9. Sometimes you've just got to do what you've got to do.
10. We have two ears and only one mouth, so listen more than you talk.
11. Believing that you can is half the journey to actually succeeding.
12. Just because you feel something now doesn't mean you will feel this way forever.
13. Nothing is ever perfect or turns out exactly like you'd hoped it would. Life is about compromise—a give-and-take that requires grace and patience. You can't have it all your own way.
14. You earn respect, you don't demand it.
15. Friendship is a two-way street—it runs both ways. Selfish people take without giving back and drain your energy, so learn to spot them and you'll save yourself a lot of time and trouble.
16. Just because you're angry or sad doesn't mean you have the right to make others feel that way.
17. Only ask the questions you honestly want

to hear the answers to, and this includes "How are you?" and "Do I look fat in this?"

18. People only bully because they're unhappy within themselves. Strong, happy people don't bully.
19. No matter how sad or angry you feel, you're still responsible for your actions.
20. Focus on your good not your bad points. It's much more constructive.
21. It's not right to be nice to someone one day and then wish him or her away the next.
22. We're given the gift of free will, the free will to think and choose for ourselves—that's what separates us from animals. Exercise your free will.
23. Always acknowledge your emotions. They serve a purpose and should never be ignored. Don't bottle them up inside where they can go bad.
24. When the going gets tough, you can either roll over and play dead, or you can rise to the challenge and take a few knocks, but emerge stronger and wiser for it.
25. Think before you talk.
26. How you treat others is a reflection of how you feel about yourself.

27. There are times when you must accept the things you cannot change; otherwise you'll just waste good time and energy trying to change them.
28. Never, ever lie to yourself. It's all too easy to believe your own lies, and once you start, you'll soon forget where the truth begins and where it ends, which will cause trouble in all shapes and colors.
29. You are responsible for your own happiness, and it all comes down to a positive attitude and making the right choices.
30. The price of greatness is responsibility. (Winston Churchill actually said that one, but it's excellent Good Sense logic.)
31. You can get through anything if you have people who care about you. It doesn't matter who, just as long as you have someone.
32. Liking yourself is far more important than being liked by other people.
33. Never laugh at anyone's dreams.
34. Sometimes you just can't help the way you feel. The best you can do is swallow it down and try to avoid doing or saying anything you might regret later, when those irky

feelings have long gone and faded. This is considering the consequences of your actions.

35. You only have to make a mistake once to learn the lesson.
36. Spend some time alone every day.
37. Don't follow a *sorry* with a *but*.
38. It's easy to take the ones you love for granted and just presume they'll always be around, but it's a big mistake.
39. Things that seem too good to be true usually aren't true at all.
40. No matter what happens or how bad it seems today, life does go on, and things will get better.
41. A good angle to approach any problem is a try-angle.
42. Change is inevitable—there's not much we can do about that. The trick is to open your arms to it but keep a firm grip on your values.
43. In life the things we most want to forget about tend to be the things we most need to talk about.
44. Don't let yesterday use up too much of today. (Cherokee Indian proverb)

45. Better safe than sorry.
46. It takes a big person to apologize, so accept the words graciously.
47. The only way to start is to start!

If you or anyone you know have been affected by any of the issues raised in this book, the following information, websites, and helplines may prove useful:

Bipolar disorder is a manic depressive illness. It is a mood disorder and can cause a person's mood to swing from very, very high to very, very low. When this happens, it can often interfere with a person's daily life. However, bipolar disorder can be treated effectively, and therefore many people live normal, healthy lives while managing the illness. It is quite a common condition—around one in one hundred people suffer from bipolar disorder.

The National Institute of Mental Health

The National Institute of Mental Health (NIMH) offers a detailed explanation of bipolar disorder, along with information about symptoms, causes, and treatments.
Website: www.nimh.nih.gov

National Suicide Hotlines

The U.S. National Suicide Hotlines have crisis counselors available twenty-four hours a day, seven days a week.
1-800-SUICIDE
1-800-784-2433
1-800-273-TALK
1-800-273-8255
Website:
http://suicidehotlines.com/national

Here are some other websites to visit to help with various isssues affecting teens today:

www.safeyouth.org
www.teenadviceonline.org
www.yellowribbon.org

About the Author

Amber Deckers grew up in South Africa, where she studied film before going on to work for an advertising agency. During this time, she studied journalism part-time and eventually joined *Marie Claire* as a features and fashion writer and book reviewer.

Deciding to swap the shores of Africa for London, Amber worked for various publishers in London before joining an independent film production company with the idea of creating a television program about teenager issues. When the project was shelved, Amber decided to put her research and ideas into a novel, which is where this book came from.

Amber and her husband, Craig, have recently returned to the UK after living in Grenada. They now live on a farm in Kent with their Doberman, Blue, and Calypso, their tabby—both rescue animals from the West Indies. Amber works as a freelance journalist and is putting the finishing touches on her next novel.